'Thank you for the barbecue,' Catherine said when they reached her car.

It was quiet here at the front of the house, away from the music and the sound of voices and laughter in the garden.

'Not at all,' he replied. 'It was nice that you could join us. But we can't impose on any more of your time. No doubt your company is greatly in demand.'

'Not really…'

'But you said you had to go. I imagined you would be meeting someone special.'

'No.' She shook her head again, suddenly acutely aware of his closeness as he held the car door open for her. 'There's no one special.'

'I find that hard to believe.' He spoke softly, but there was something different, some new element that ha

Laura MacDonald was born and bred on the Isle of Wight and lives there now with her husband. Her daughter is a nurse and her son is an actor and she has a young grandson. The lovely Isle of Wight scenery has provided the setting for many of Laura's books. When she is not writing for Harlequin Mills & Boon® she writes children's books under the name Carol Barton.

Recent titles by the same author:

MEDIC ON APPROVAL
A KIND OF MAGIC

THE SURGEON'S DILEMMA

BY
LAURA MacDONALD

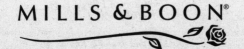

MILLS & BOON®

First published in Great Britain 2001
Harlequin Mills & Boon Limited,
Eton House, 18-24 Paradise Road, Richmond, Surrey TW9 1SR

© Laura MacDonald 2001

ISBN 0 263 82680 5

Set in Times Roman 10½ on 12 pt.
03-0801-46913

Printed and bound in Spain
by Litografia Rosés, S.A., Barcelona

CHAPTER ONE

'WELL, now, don't you think he's just the dreamiest man you ever saw?'

'Who?' Staff Nurse Catherine Slade straightened up from tidying Marion Finch's bedcovers in readiness for the morning ward round.

'Him.' Marion nodded towards the nurses' station beyond the four-bedded bay where she was awaiting her operation.

Catherine glanced over her shoulder and saw the group of doctors talking to Sister Marlow. 'D'you mean Simon Andrews, our houseman?'

'No.' Marion shook her head. 'He's nice, I grant you, but he's still wet behind the ears. No, I mean him—Mr Grantham.'

'Oh, really?' Catherine looked a bit startled. 'To tell you the truth, I hadn't really noticed.'

'Oh, you young nurses.' Marion Finch sighed and rolled her eyes. 'You can't see what's under your eyes. On the other hand, I dare say you're a bit young...although, having said that, you shouldn't be deceived by that hair of his. I would say that's definitely a case of premature greying. I find it very attractive myself...especially with those eyes. Don't tell me you haven't noticed his eyes!'

'Actually, no.' Catherine shook her head but she was laughing now. 'What you must remember, Marion, is that I'm very new here—I hardly know anyone. And the other thing is that Mr Grantham is way out of my

5

league. He's "the Boss" around here and I doubt he knows us lowly little staff nurses even exist.'

'He's probably married as well,' said Marion gloomily. 'They always are. But there's no harm in fantasising, I suppose. Oh, here they come.'

They fell silent as the doctors approached Marion's bed and Catherine stood back.

Sister Marlow took a folder of notes from the trolley and handed them to Mr Grantham. He, however, had already turned his full attention to Marion Finch.

'We meet again, Mrs Finch,' he said, without waiting for a reminder from Sister. His voice was authoritative but quiet and beautifully modulated. 'How have you been?'

'Not too bad, Mr Grantham,' Marion replied, 'but I'll be glad when today's over.'

'I'm sure you will because I'm about to make a new woman of you.' He smiled and Catherine noticed with amusement that Marion's cheeks had grown quite pink. As Sister passed over the records Catherine found herself leaning forward slightly to see if she could see Mr Grantham's eyes. His gaze, however, was on the notes and after a moment she gave up the attempt.

'The consultant anaesthetist will be along to see you shortly, Mrs Finch,' said Mr Grantham. 'Meanwhile…' he closed the folder and handed it back to Sister '…I will prepare for our next meeting, which will be in Theatre. You, of course, may not be aware of that so I will perform your hysterectomy and come back to see you tomorrow.'

'Thank you, Mr Grantham,' breathed Marion. 'Thank you very much.'

It was at that moment that Catherine became aware that someone was watching her. She moved her head and her gaze met that of Senior House Officer Simon Andrews. When he saw he had attracted her attention he winked. Carefully she redirected her gaze but not before she had allowed the slightest of smiles to tug at her mouth.

It was time then for the consultant gynaecologist and his entourage to move on to the next patient.

'I could die happy now.' Marion gave a deep sigh.

'You don't really mean that, Marion,' said Catherine with a chuckle.

'Don't I?' Marion grinned. 'No, I don't suppose I do. And, really, I wouldn't change my Derek for the world—but, well, there's no harm in a girl dreaming, is there?'

Catherine left Marion then and made her way back to the nurses' station. Sister had already told her she had an admission she wanted her to do that morning, and a glance at the clock showed that the patient would be arriving at any moment. Senior Staff Nurse Lizzie Rowe was at the desk in the nurses' station and she looked up as Catherine approached.

'How's it going?' she asked.

'All right, I think.' Catherine nodded. 'Gradually getting to know people's names.'

'It all takes time—after all, you've only been here three days.' Lizzie paused. 'Is Marion Finch ready for Theatre?'

'Yes.' Catherine nodded. 'Just waiting for the anaesthetist now, then she can have her pre-med. I must say she seems very taken with Mr Grantham.'

'All his patients are. He seems to have the knack of making them feel they are the only one he has to deal with.'

'Sometimes that sort of thing comes across as over-familiarity,' observed Catherine.

'Not in Paul Grantham's case. His conduct is too correct for that. Oh, here's the anaesthetist now...' Lizzie trailed off as a slightly built man approached the desk.

'Ah.' The man leaned across the counter and beamed at Catherine. 'We have a new face in the camp. How do you do?'

'Catherine, this is Mr Patel,' said Lizzie. 'I don't think you've met him yet. He's been on leave.'

'No, I don't believe I have...' Catherine smiled. 'Pleased to meet you, Mr Patel.'

'Oh, please, please, call me Sanjay...everyone does.'

'He's lovely,' said Lizzie as Sanjay bustled away onto the ward. 'We all tend to forget he's a consultant—he's one of us, if you know what I mean.'

'Not like Mr Grantham, then?'

'How do you mean?' Lizzie frowned.

'Well, would you call him Paul?'

'Lord, no! He's a bit like God around here.'

'That's what I mean,' said Catherine, but Lizzie wasn't listening. She was answering the phone. While she was talking a porter suddenly appeared and handed Catherine two large boxes.

'Where do these go?' asked Catherine as Lizzie came off the phone.

'Oh, under the counter. See if you can make a space for them. It's only some folders and envelopes and things that we'd run out of. Oh, and watch the desk for a moment, will you? I need the loo.'

'OK.' Catherine crouched down and began making some space on a shelf. She had almost finished when she became aware that someone was standing at the desk, but because she was at floor level she was unable to see who it was. 'Can I help you?' she called. Attempting to stand up, she caught her heel in the hem of her dress and almost toppled backwards. It wasn't until she had regained her balance that she finally looked up at the person who was standing at the desk. Her gaze met a pair of incredibly blue eyes, eyes that made an unusual and startling contrast to the owner's silver-grey hair.

'Are you all right?' he asked quietly, and for the briefest of moments she thought she detected a note of concern in that beautifully modulated tone, but at the same time she felt foolish at behaving in so ungainly a manner in front of him.

'Yes, thank you. I caught my heel…'

'I need to use a phone.'

'Oh, please, any of them…' Wildly she indicated the phones on the desk.

'Thank you.' He picked up a receiver and began dialling numbers. Catherine, suddenly mindful of Marion Finch's observations of this man, found her eyes drawn to his hands. Fine hands. Surgeon's hands with long fingers, their tips slightly squared. He glanced up and saw her watching him. Suddenly confused, she hurriedly looked away.

'Catherine, your admission has just arrived.'

It was Sister Marlow speaking to her, and Catherine found she was glad of the diversion for she found the incident with the consultant gynaecologist, brief as it had been, in some way disconcerting.

The patient for admission was Edna McBride, a single lady in her late sixties who had come into hospital with a vaginal prolapse. Catherine showed her into the small interview room where admissions were carried out. 'I need to ask you some questions, Miss McBride.'

Edna McBride sat down, arranging her sensible tweed skirt so that it covered her knees. 'More questions?' She raised her eyebrows.

'Most things were probably covered at your pre-op assessment,' said Catherine, 'but we do need to make sure that nothing has changed since then. Now, I see from your notes that you're taking medication for hypertension and recurrent bladder infections. Have you brought that medication with you?'

Edna McBride nodded and took two, small, neatly labelled bottles from her handbag. 'I've taken the nifedipine tablet for my blood pressure this morning and one of the antibiotics. I need to take another antibiotic tonight.'

'Thank you.' Catherine took the bottles from her. 'I'll put those on the drugs trolley and you'll be given your medication at the appropriate times.'

'I sometimes need to take an indigestion tablet so I've brought those with me as well.'

Catherine duly noted the name of the tablets and entered the information in the patient's notes. 'Your operation will take place tomorrow, Edna—I may call you Edna?' Catherine usually automatically called patients by their first names but something about Miss McBride's manner made her feel compelled to ask first.

'If you must.' Edna McBride replied in a resigned voice, then after a slight pause she said, 'It *will* be Mr Grantham who performs my operation, won't it?'

'Well, he was the consultant you saw in outpatients,' Catherine replied checking her notes, 'so it's almost certain it will be him.'

'What do you mean, almost certain?' Edna McBride

peered fiercely at Catherine over the top of her spectacles.

'There's sometimes the chance that Mr Grantham's registrar, Dr Prowse, has to take over an operation…'

'Why?'

'Well, if Mr Grantham is detained on another case, for example, or if he has to perform an emergency operation.'

'I see. Well, let's hope that isn't the case.' Edna pursed her lips. 'I trust Mr Grantham explicitly and I want him to perform my operation.'

'And I'm sure it will be him,' Catherine replied soothingly.

'Do I see him before the operation?' asked Edna.

Catherine nodded. 'Yes, he will be along to see you later today and the anaesthetist will also come in to see you. Have you had any previous operations?'

'I had an operation for an ovarian cyst but that was over twenty-five years ago.'

'I'm sure you will find that many procedures have changed since then.'

'Yes, I dare say they have, and not all for the better either,' Edna replied crisply.

'No, well, we do our best,' said Catherine.

'I dare say you do.' Edna seemed to soften slightly.

'Now, if I could just take your blood pressure and check your height and weight, I'll show you to your bed.'

'I don't have to get into bed now, do I? I'm not used to lazing around.'

'I'm sure you're not,' Catherine replied with a smile. 'But you need to rest before your operation and it will be easier for the doctors to examine you if you're in bed.'

'Oh, very well.'

When Catherine returned to the nurses' station, after completing Edna McBride's admission and making sure she was comfortably installed in bed, Lizzie Rowe met her and suggested the two of them go off to the staff canteen for their coffee-break.

'That's the best idea I've heard all morning,' said Catherine with a grin.

'New patient all right?' asked Lizzie as the two of them left Gynae and walked down the corridor together.

Catherine nodded. 'A bit fierce. Retired school-teacher apparently. Knows exactly what she wants and what she doesn't want, and thinks hospitals should be run the same way as they were twenty-five years ago.'

'Maybe she has a point,' Lizzie replied with a sigh.

'Oh, I don't know,' said Catherine as they reached the canteen and pushed open the doors, 'my mum was a nurse and she used to say she remembers being terrorised by their matron—I wouldn't care for that.'

'No, I suppose not,' Lizzie agreed.

They collected coffee and biscuits from the self-service counter and found a table near the window.

'Is your mum still in nursing?' asked Lizzie as she removed the Cellophane wrapping from her biscuits.

'No.' Catherine shook her head, aware of the thud that always hit her whenever she spoke of her mother. 'She's dead now,' she added quietly.

'Oh, I'm sorry,' said Lizzie, her eyes widening in surprise. 'She must have been young.'

'Forty-six. She had a brain tumour. It was all very sudden. But that was three years ago now. I was working in Oxford at the time. Mum was living here in Langbury.'

'So, did you ever live in Langbury?'

'Yes. I was born and brought up here,' Catherine replied. 'I went to Oxford to do my training then after I'd qualified I worked in the same hospital for a further five years. A year on Accident and Emergency and four years on Gynae.'

'And now you've come home to Langbury.'

Catherine smiled. 'Yes, now I've come home to Langbury. I always meant to. I'd planned to some years ago but after Mum died somehow there didn't seem much point...'

'Your father—is he...?'

'No, he's very much alive, but he lives in London. He and my mother were divorced and he married again some years before she died.'

'So do you have other family here?'

'Some,' Catherine replied. 'An aunt and a couple of cousins, but my roots are here in Langbury. I went to school here, I have friends here and...'

'Do I detect there might be someone special here who prompted your need to return?' asked Lizzie quizzically.

'No, not at all.' Catherine shrugged. 'There hasn't really been anyone for a couple of years or so now. He was a SHO in Oxford but it didn't really work out. I think it was a bit soon after my mum dying. That hit me hard and I wasn't ready for any intense relationships.'

'So what was your other reason for coming here?'

'My other reason?' Catherine frowned.

'Yes, I got the impression you were about to say there was something else apart from roots and family.'

'Did you? Well, yes, I suppose there is in a way. When I lived here before I was a member of the

Langbury Amateur Dramatic Society—the LADS, as they are fondly known as.'

'I've heard of them,' said Lizzie. 'They put on some really good productions.'

'Yes, their standard is very high,' Catherine agreed. 'Anyway I've joined up again.'

'Oh, great. Are you in anything at the moment?'

'Well, they're doing *Oliver!* for their summer production but they had already done the casting so I was too late. But there will be others, and I'm going to help out backstage with this one.'

'I'm sure they'll be glad of your help. What's your speciality?'

'I like it all,' Catherine admitted. 'Acting, singing. I've even tried my hand at a bit of directing.'

'Well, I think that's wonderful—and a good way of getting to know people.' Lizzie paused. 'Where are you living?'

'I've got myself a cottage in Priory Road.'

'I know them.' Lizzie nodded. 'They are lovely old places down there.'

Catherine nodded. 'It needs a bit doing to it—but all in good time. Anyway, that's enough about me—what about you? Where do you live?'

'I'm in one of the houses up on the new estate at Langbury Heights.'

'Are you married?'

'No.' Lizzie shook her head. 'I live with my boyfriend. We'll probably get around to getting married one day—but not yet. Which reminds me, I need to give him a ring. Excuse me a minute—I'll be back.' She stood up and hurried across the canteen to the payphone in the far corner.

Catherine sat back in her chair and sipped her coffee.

She liked working with Lizzie who had gone out of her way to be kind to her ever since she'd started on Gynae. In fact, if she was honest, she was beginning to like most things about her new job. She'd had a few doubts about returning to Langbury. You can't go back, people had said, it's never the same. Well, maybe it wasn't the same but, then, Catherine wasn't at all certain that she wanted it to be. New job, new home, new friends—that was what she needed and that was what was happening.

'We meet again.'

She looked up sharply, jolted out of her daydreaming, to find Simon Andrews looking down at her with a smile on his face.

'Mind if I join you?'

'Be my guest.' Catherine nodded towards an empty chair. 'But I have to be back on the ward in about five minutes.'

'Story of my life,' said Simon with a sigh. 'I find a pretty, lonely girl and she tells me she has to be somewhere else.'

'Who says I'm lonely?'

'You looked lonely.'

'Did I?'

'Well, perhaps not lonely—pensive. Yes, that's the word—pensive. Pensive but vulnerable, as if you needed someone to take care of you.'

'Don't listen to him, Catherine.' Suddenly Lizzie was back. 'He has a store of chat-up lines the likes of which you simply wouldn't believe.'

'Oh, I don't know.' Catherine laughed then, draining her cup, she rose to her feet. 'I quite liked the idea of being pensive but vulnerable, and the idea of someone taking care of me certainly has its attractions.'

'Is that what he said?' spluttered Lizzie. 'Oh, Simon, I do believe you're losing your touch.'

'Don't you believe it,' Simon replied. 'Catherine will remember me, won't you, Catherine?' He looked up at her appealingly.

'How could I forget?' She pressed her hand to her heart.

'So, you see, it had the desired effect.' He grinned at Lizzie.

'Come on, Catherine, we can't stay listening to this nonsense. We have people on that ward who really need us.'

The two staff nurses made their way out of the canteen and back to Gynae. 'Is he always like that?' Catherine threw Liz a sidelong glance.

'*Always*,' Liz replied. 'And I'm not sure I'd recommend him if you're looking for a relationship.'

'Who says I'm looking for a relationship?'

'Just wondered, that's all. Seeing that you said there's no man in your life at present.'

'Actually, believe it or not, I'm quite happy on my own,' she replied briskly. As they reached the ward and pushed open the double doors they were forced to wait, holding the door, as someone came up behind them. With a little start Catherine realised it was Mr Grantham. They stood aside as with a brief incline of his head in acknowledgement he passed them, heading towards Sister's office. 'But that's not to say,' she went on thoughtfully, 'that if the right man came along I wouldn't be interested.' Her eyes were still on the consultant gynaecologist's retreating back as she spoke.

'I hope you're not referring to him,' said Lizzie drily. 'He's what's known as an untouchable.'

'Yes, I dare say.' Catherine nodded.

'He is attractive, though,' Lizzie added. 'I grant you that. Not that he'd ever look twice at the likes of us lowly minions.'

'No. I suppose not,' Catherine agreed.

By the time they reached the nurses' station and had taken over from the two other duty staff nurses, the phone was ringing. As Lizzie picked up the receiver Mr Grantham and Sister Marlow came out of the office.

'I really need to go and get scrubbed up,' he said, glancing at his watch. 'But I'll just have a word with Miss McBride before I do. Perhaps you'd like to accompany me, Sister?'

'Sister, Nursing Officer on the phone for you.' Lizzie held out the receiver to Glenda Marlow, who glanced helplessly at Mr Grantham.

'It's all right,' he said swiftly. 'I'll go on my own.'

'Staff nurse Slade will accompany you,' Sister replied as she took the receiver from Lizzie.

Together Catherine and Mr Grantham made their way onto the ward and into the four-bedded section where Edna McBride was sitting up in bed, knitting.

She looked up as they approached. 'Oh, Mr Grantham.' She lowered her needles and Catherine was amused to see that she looked slightly flustered.

'Hello, Miss McBride.' Mr Grantham stopped beside the bed. 'This isn't an official visit—I'll be along later or possibly in the morning to talk to you about your operation. But Sister Marlow has told me that you're very anxious about who will be performing your surgery.'

'Well, yes, I am,' Edna McBride admitted. 'I understood all along that it would be you and then I was informed there was a chance that it could be your registrar.'

'There is always a slight chance of that,' Paul Grantham agreed. 'But let me reassure you…' As he spoke he leaned forward and covered her hand with his. 'God willing, it will be me performing your surgery in the morning.'

'Oh, thank you. Thank you, Mr Grantham. You've no idea how you've put my mind at rest.'

'Not at all.' He straightened up. 'Now, you get some rest and I'll see you later.' He glanced at Catherine. 'Thank you, Staff Nurse,' he said, and fleetingly it crossed Catherine's mind that he had no idea that she was the same nurse who had acted in such an ungainly manner in front of him only a couple of hours earlier. No doubt all nurses looked the same to him. But it was true what Lizzie had said, he really was very attractive. Immaculately dressed in a charcoal grey, pinstriped suit with a crisp white shirt, the combination of his hair and those blue eyes really was quite devastating.

Catherine escorted him back to the nurses' station where, after a quick word with Sister, he left for the theatre and the busy ward routine resumed.

'Did Mr Grantham come up especially to see Edna McBride?' asked Lizzie curiously a little later as she and Catherine met briefly in the sluice room.

'Apparently so. She was worried about the fact that it might not be him doing her op. He came to reassure her.'

'See what I mean about him making his patients feel special?' said Lizzie.

Catherine nodded. 'I have to say I haven't come across that with too many other consultants—at least, not to that degree.' She glanced out of the sluice as she spoke. 'Oh, here come the porters to take Marion Finch down to Theatre—I must go.' Leaving Lizzie in the sluice, she hurried back onto the ward.

Marion was drowsy from her pre-med but it didn't stop her chattering about anything and everything to Catherine and the porters all the way to Theatre. It was only when she was wheeled into the anaesthetics room and they were met by the theatre sister that she seemed anxious and clung tightly to Catherine's hand.

'It's all right, Marion,' Catherine said. 'I have to go now, but you'll be fine. I'm going to leave you with Sister.'

'You will be there when I come round?' murmured Marion.

'Of course. I'll see you later.'

'OK.' Marion nodded. 'Mr Grantham,' she mumbled, 'I'm all yours.'

'That's what they all say,' said the theatre sister as she came into the anaesthetics room. Behind her, briefly, through the open doors Catherine caught a glimpse of a figure clad in theatre greens, a figure who would have been indistingishable from any other in Theatre but for the distinctive blue of his eyes above his mask.

CHAPTER TWO

WITH the help of care assistant Eileen Swan, Catherine received Marion Finch back from Theatre, transferring her from the porters' trolley to a clean, warm bed. She then carried out the necessary post op observations of blood pressure, pulse and temperature and checked the saline and blood transfusions that Marion was receiving. The two nurses proceeded to give Marion a bed bath to make her more comfortable and used swabs to freshen her mouth. Catherine checked that Marion's catheter was functioning properly.

'We've nearly finished with you, Marion,' said Catherine as Marion gave a groan. 'I'm going to give you an injection for the pain then you can get some rest.' Throughout all these procedures Marion had remained very drowsy. When they were over, Eileen combed her hair then laid her gently back onto her pillows where she promptly fell fast asleep again.

As Catherine tidied up and Eileen hurried off to the sluice room, Catherine saw that Lizzie and care assistant Tiffany Roberts had received another patient back from Theatre, a young woman who had been experiencing infertility problems and who had also been on Mr Grantham's theatre list for that day. Out of the corner of her eye, in passing, she also saw that Sanjay Patel was talking to Edna McBride and appeared to be making her laugh.

At last Catherine's shift was over and she made her way to the nurses' staffroom where she changed from her uniform into a long, grey, ribbed skirt and a pink, cotton, polonecked sweater. Moving to the mirror, she took her comb from her bag. She'd recently had her dark hair cut short and was still faintly surprised each time she looked in the mirror and caught sight of her unfamiliar reflection. She had been told that the style suited her but that had been by people who hadn't known her before when she had worn her hair shoulder length.

Large, expressive brown eyes gazed back at her as critically she tilted her head and, as she always did, wished that her mouth wasn't quite so wide. With a sigh she ran the comb through her hair before returning it to her bag. Then, after applying a touch of lipstick, she headed for the door.

Outside in the hospital grounds she took several deep breaths before heading for the car park. Her rather elderly little Renault was tucked away in a corner and as she stopped beside it, fumbling in her bag for her keys, her attention was briefly taken by a large, dark grey Jaguar that was reversing out of a space opposite. She might not have spared it a second glance—after all, there was nothing unusual or significant about the car—but as it purred softly past her Catherine caught a glimpse of the driver and there *was* something about Paul Grantham that was both unusual and significant.

He didn't see her, or if he had he gave no indication of the fact. Not that there was anything unusual about that either. Consultant surgeons didn't usually go out of their way to acknowledge members of the nursing staff.

Catherine unlocked her car door, slipped into the driver's seat and found herself wondering about Paul Grantham. No doubt he was disgustingly rich, lived in a great mansion of a house, had a beautiful, blonde trophy wife and several equally beautiful children who were all intelligent and athletic and who were destined to become consultants or barristers in their turn. Not like the rest of us who live in the real world, she thought grimly as she switched on the engine and drew out of the car park.

Since coming back to Langbury, Catherine had had to battle to secure a mortgage on her cottage and had fought long and hard with local services and contractors who had promised to come then had failed to turn up. All this had been followed by one hassle after another, from wrong goods being delivered to a leaking washing machine and a faulty shower attachment.

But in spite of all that she was pleased with her cottage and didn't for one moment regret buying it. It would be a struggle on her salary, she didn't doubt that, but the small legacy her mother had left her had helped with a deposit, and at least, the place was hers. No more pleading with landlords to put things right or begging to change decor as she had been forced to do in the past in the succession of rented accommodation she'd had since starting nursing.

The cottage, situated to the east of Langbury in a narrow lane leading to the old priory, was the middle one in a terrace of five. Colour-washed in pale green with darker green window-frames and door, its garden overflowed with flowering shrubs and plants. To Catherine's delight there was even a small kitchen garden at the rear packed with mint, chives, basil and rosemary. The neighbours had been friendly and welcoming and the elderly couple in the bungalow opposite had even said Catherine could park her car on their drive as they no longer owned a car.

And it still held a thrill at the end of each day to put her key in the cottage door and as it swung open to be greeted by her cat, Teazer, who ran to meet her.

'Hello, you old softie.' Bending down, in one movement she fondled the large fluffy black and white cat and picked up her post which had been delivered after she'd left for work that morning.

It was good to be home and, after feeding Teazer, Catherine took a shower then prepared a light meal for herself before getting ready to leave for the theatre and a rehearsal for *Oliver!*

The theatre where the LADS performed all their productions was situated in the heart of Langbury in the park beside the river. It was a modern building, but not lacking in charm, and it provided an ideal location for the many and varied productions that took place there throughout the year. Catherine had been sorry that she had been too late for the casting of *Oliver!*, but she was only too willing to help in whatever area she could and already there had been talk of the next production being *My Fair Lady*. It had been suggested that she should audition for the part of Eliza Doolittle.

Catherine had been involved in amateur theatre for as long as she could remember. Her father had been an entertainer and everyone had said that Catherine had inherited her talent from him. She had been taught to sing and to dance at a very early age and had enjoyed every production she had taken part in.

She'd been welcomed back into LADS with open arms on her return to Langbury, and her various skills and talents had quickly been put to use.

For that evening's rehearsal she found herself in the stalls alongside the director, Rod Janes, as the cast ran through the show's various musical numbers. One young girl, who was playing the part of the flower-seller in the street scene, seemed to be having difficulty with the song 'Who Will Buy?'

'Her voice is breathtaking,' murmured Rod, 'but her timing is all wrong. Do you think you could help her with it, Catherine?'

'I can try.' Catherine nodded. 'What's her name?'

'Abbie,' Rod replied. 'She's new with us this season.'

Catherine made a note on her pad to speak to the girl after the rehearsal, then looked up, preparing to concentrate on the big scene between the couple playing Nancy and Bill Sykes—two of the principal leads in *Oliver!*

After the rehearsal she made her way to the dressing room where she found Abbie packing her music into a small rucksack.

'Abbie?' she said. Startled, the girl looked up. Catherine was struck by two things—the girl's lovely eyes, so deep in colour they appeared almost violet, and the fact that at close quarters, with her blonde hair caught up into a topknot, she looked younger than she had on stage. 'Rod has asked me to have a word with you about your song.'

'I was rubbish, wasn't I? He doesn't want me any more—that's it, isn't it?'

'Not at all,' said Catherine hurriedly, knowing from experience how the girl must be feeling. 'You weren't rubbish—you were very good. You have a lovely voice but we feel you need a bit of extra help with timing and breathing—that sort of thing.'

Abbie frowned. 'So what can I do?'

'Do you have singing lessons with anyone?'

Catherine was more than willing to help the girl but she didn't want to tread on anyone's toes.

Abbie shook her head.

'In that case maybe you could come half an hour earlier to the next few rehearsals and we'll run through some voice exercises together with your number. Would that be all right?'

'Oh, yes.' The violet eyes suddenly lit up. 'That would be great. Thank you. Thank you very much.'

'I'm Catherine, by the way. I'm not actually in this production because I've only just rejoined the society. I used to belong a few years ago,' Catherine explained when she saw Abbie's puzzled expression, 'but I moved away.'

Abbie finished packing her bag and Catherine walked out of the dressing room with her. Together they made their way through the rabbit warren of back-stage corridors to the stage door.

'Have you been in a lot of shows?' Abbie asked, throwing her a sidelong glance.

'A few,' Catherine admitted. '*Carousel*, *Half a Sixpence*. Oh, and I played Sandie in *Grease*.'

'Did you?' breathed Abbie in awe.

'Yes, complete with blonde wig.'

'I'd love to play Sandie…'

'You will one day. With a voice like yours, I shouldn't wonder you'd soon be playing the West End. Now,' she went on as Abbie flushed, 'don't forget, half an hour earlier next time.'

As Abbie left the theatre Catherine caught sight of Rod and briefly told him what she had arranged.

'Bless you, Catherine,' he said. 'You're a star.'

After leaving Rod, Catherine herself left the theatre, and as she was walking from the stage door to the car park she was briefly dazzled by the lights of a car leaving. She stepped aside as the large, dark-coloured car swept past. The car was a Jaguar, reminding Catherine briefly of Paul Grantham's car—not that there could be any connection between the two, of course. There must be many Jaguars in Langbury, even large, dark grey, expensive-looking ones.

The following morning Edna McBride went to Theatre for her prolapse operation. Catherine accompanied her and it was only when they were actually in the anaesthetics room that Catherine realised that not only was the former schoolteacher nervous, which would have been understandable, but that she was actually very nervous indeed.

'It's all right,' Catherine murmured as Edna clung to her hand. 'It'll soon be all over now and you'll feel so much better afterwards.'

'It *is* Mr Grantham today, isn't it?' whispered Edna, holding onto Catherine's hand even more tightly.

'I'll check for you.' Gently Catherine extricated her hand and, moving forward, tried to see into the area beyond the anaesthetics room.

'Is there a problem?' The theatre sister bustled up behind her.

'No, not really.' Catherine shook her head. 'I just wanted to check that it is Mr Grantham operating this morning. Miss McBride is very anxious that it should be him.'

Sister didn't even have the chance to reply for another voice intervened—a deeper voice, a male voice, its tone instantly recognisable. 'I was about to reassure Miss McBride.'

Catherine looked up quickly and found herself looking once again into those incredibly blue eyes. For a fraction of a second something stirred in her memory, something indefinable, some memory or recognition, then it was gone, leaving Catherine wondering if she had imagined it. His mask had not yet been positioned and was lying loosely around his neck so the strong jawline and finely chiselled features were clearly visible.

Catherine noticed his skin was tanned, which conjured up images of lazy days on some Mediterranean beach and threw the colour of his hair and his eyes into even greater contrast.

'Thank you,' she heard herself say. 'She'll appreciate that.'

The faintest of smiles touched his lips and he moved across the room to stand beside Edna and speak soft but reassuring words. Catherine couldn't hear what he said but after he moved away and back into Theatre she found Edna in a far more relaxed frame of mind than she had been only moments before.

Catherine returned to the ward where she was met by Sister Marlow who informed her that her new admission had just arrived and was waiting for her in the interview room. 'Her name is Helen Brooker,' she added.

Catherine nodded. 'Total hysterectomy, isn't it?'

'That's right.' Sister handed her the patient's record folder and Catherine briefly glanced through it. 'She's very young for a total.'

Glenda Marlow nodded. 'She had a positive smear test followed by an equally positive cone biopsy. Mr Grantham is hoping that this measure will be all that is required.'

'She has children, hasn't she?' Catherine frowned as she looked up from the notes.

'Yes, three.'

'Well, I'd better get on with it.'

Helen Brooker was sitting in the interview room, flicking through the pages of a glossy magazine. She looked up sharply as Catherine came into the room and Catherine was struck by the woman's fresh, natural complexion and smooth hair which was cut into an attractive bob.

'Hello,' said Catherine brightly. 'Helen Brooker?'

The woman nodded. She was slightly built with large, rather anxious, hazel eyes. 'Yes, that's right.' She pushed the magazine away. She appeared nervous and began twisting her hands together in her lap.

'I'm Staff Nurse Catherine Slade. I'm to do your admission so I need to take some details from you. There are rather a lot of routine questions, I'm afraid.'

'That's OK.'

Catherine sat down at the table, opened her folder and proceeded to take down Helen Brooker's personal details, before turning to her medical history.

'Have you ever had a serious illness?'

Helen shook her head. 'Not really. At least not what you'd call serious. The usual childhood things— chickenpox, mumps...'

'What about operations?'

'I had my tonsils out when I was eleven.'

'Anything since?'

'No, not until the biopsy.'

'OK. Now, how many pregnancies have you had?' Catherine glanced up.

'I have three children,' Helen replied, and the pride

was obvious in her eyes. 'Two boys and a girl,' she added. 'They are eight, six and four.'

'Any miscarriages or terminations?'

'I had a miscarriage first, before I had Joe.'

'Right.' Catherine entered the details on the form. 'Now,' she went on, 'you know that your operation is to be a total hysterectomy—do you understand what that means?'

'That they'll take the cervix as well as the womb and the ovaries,' Helen replied quietly. 'Mr Grantham explained that to me. He said it was a precautionary measure. The cancer was already in my cervix but hopefully this will stop it spreading any further.'

Catherine looked up again, suddenly grateful that Paul Grantham had explained things so satisfactorily, then she saw that there were tears in Helen Brooker's eyes.

Catherine carried on making notes in order to give Helen a chance to compose herself. 'Is there anything you want to ask me?' she asked gently at last.

'Yes.' Helen nodded. 'About afterwards, after the operation…will I have drips and things?'

'Yes,' Catherine replied. 'You will have a saline drip and possibly you will have a blood transfusion. There will be a drain in place as well. You will also have a catheter, at least when you first come back from Theatre.'

'It all sounds horrendous.' Helen pulled a face.

'All those things are there to help you. The saline drip is to prevent you becoming dehydrated which in itself can be very distressing. The blood will be to re-place any you may have lost during the operation, the drain is to get rid of any waste fluids from the wound and the catheter stops you having to worry about calling for a bedpan every time you want to wee.'

Helen managed a smile. 'Well, I suppose when you put it like that it all sounds different.' She paused. 'What about the pain?'

'It will be very well controlled, Helen. You need have no fears about that. You will be given a pre-med to relax you a couple of hours or so before the op, then when you come round you will be given strong pain-killers that will probably send you straight back to sleep again.'

'My GP said I would be here for about a week. Is that right?'

'That's the average for a hysterectomy. When you get home you'll need to take things easy for a few weeks—no heavy lifting or anything like that. Is there anyone who can help you with the children?'

'Well, my husband is very good and my mum lives nearby so I'm sure we'll manage between us.'

'Is there anything else you want to ask me?'

'I don't think so…' She hesitated. 'Oh, yes, will the children be able to visit me?'

'Of course. Although Sister does restrict visitors to two to a bed and it's probably best if only your husband comes in on the evening of the operation. You'll be too tired to talk much anyway. Now, if you're happy with all that I'll take you along to your bed where I shall need to check your temperature, pulse and blood pressure. I shall then want you to do a specimen of urine for me.'

'Will I see Mr Grantham before my operation?' Helen stood up and followed Catherine from the interview room.

'Yes, he'll be along to see you later and also Mr

Patel, the anaesthetist, will want to examine you.' Catherine stopped. 'Now, this is your bed. Your locker is there. I'll leave you to get yourself sorted out then I'll be back in ten minutes or so to carry out those observations I was telling you about.'

Making her way to the nurses' station, Catherine met Lizzie. There was a definite smile on Lizzie's face and Catherine questioningly raised her eyebrows. 'You look happy,' she said. 'Anything to do with…? Oh, sorry, I don't even know your boyfriend's name.'

'Scott.' Lizzie's grin widened. 'And, no, as it happens, it isn't to do with him…not this time anyway. It's Rosy Saunders.'

'The blocked Fallopian tubes?'

Lizzie nodded. 'Yes. Mr Grantham has told her that he was successful in clearing her tubes and that there's no reason now why she shouldn't be able to have a baby. Her husband has just come to pick her up—they are absolutely over the moon and I shouldn't wonder if they haven't gone straight off home to get started.'

'It's great when patients go home happy, isn't it?' Catherine gave a little sigh. 'I only hope there will be a happy ending for the lady I've just admitted.'

'Who's that?' Lizzie looked over Catherine's shoulder at the patient folder in her hands. 'Oh, Helen Brooker. Yes, I remember her—she was in recently for a cone biopsy. I understand it was positive.'

'She's back now for a total hysterectomy—she says Mr Grantham told her it's a precautionary measure.'

'Let's hope it's been caught in time,' said Lizzie grimly. 'We've been seeing too many of those just lately.' She paused. 'She has young children doesn't she?'

Catherine nodded. 'Yes, three.'

'Well, miracles do happen around here, especially if Paul Grantham has anything to do with them. Oh, by the way, Scott is meeting me after work and we're going with some of the others for a drink in the pub across the road—would you like to join us?'

'I'd love to, thanks,' said Catherine. 'I won't be able to stay for too long—there's a rehearsal for *Oliver!* and I've promised to give some help to a young girl who's having difficulty with her part.'

'That's good of you.'

'Not really. It's something I love doing.' She glanced at her watch. 'Lord! I must get on. I have to do Helen Brooker's obs then receive Edna McBride back from Theatre.'

It didn't take long to complete Helen's observations and Catherine had just finished when the porters returned to the ward with Edna.

Care Assistant Eileen Swan had prepared a clean bed and, together with the porters, she and Catherine lifted Edna from the trolley.

'She was quite a time in Recovery,' said the nurse who had accompanied the porters from the theatre. 'Took rather a while to come round. But she's all right now.' She handed Catherine a chart. 'Here are her obs.'

Catherine took the chart and saw that Edna had been written up for strong pain relief and half-hourly observations.

'We'll get her comfortable,' she said to Eileen. 'A wash and freshen-up will work wonders.'

'I know it's a trial, Edna,' said Catherine sympathetically as Edna groaned, 'but you really will feel better after this, you know.' With Eileen's help, and taking care not to disturb either the saline drip or the catheter, she took off the white theatre gown which had become soiled during the operation. Together the two nurses washed Edna thoroughly then applied deodorant and some of her own freesia-scented talcum powder before helping her into a fresh, cotton nightdress.

'May I have a sip of water?' asked Edna faintly as Eileen combed her hair.

'Yes, of course you may.' Catherine filled a glass tumbler with water from the jug on Edna's locker, then supporting her head with one hand, held it to her lips.

'I need to take your blood pressure again, Edna,' said Catherine, when she had finished, 'and then, I promise you, we'll go away and leave you in peace.'

'Thank goodness for that,' Edna replied faintly.

Catherine smiled at the patient's retort. She had just finished checking her blood pressure and was removing the cuff from Edna's arm when a quiet footfall behind her made her turn. Paul Grantham, devoid of his theatre greens and now wearing a white coat, stood at the foot of the bed. Edna, by this time, had sunk back onto her pillows and had closed her eyes.

'How is she?' The consultant surgeon picked up the observation chart from the bed rail as he spoke and studied it.

'She's doing well, Mr Grantham,' Catherine replied, 'but she's very tired. I think she's asleep now.'

Edna's eyes snapped open. 'I most certainly am not asleep,' she said.

'Ah, Miss McBride.' Paul Grantham moved round to the side of the bed. 'You're back with us. You'll be pleased to know that your operation went very well and was a complete success. You shouldn't have any further problems with stress incontinence or the bladder infections you were experiencing.'

'Thank you, Mr Grantham. Thank you very much indeed.'

'It's a pleasure Miss McBride. Now, tell me, how is the pain?'

'Tolerable.'

'Good. Well, Staff Nurse here will see that it stays that way.' He glanced at Catherine as he spoke and inclined his head slightly before moving away from the bed. He was so charming to his patients but Catherine found herself wondering if he'd actually seen her, whether, if he was asked to describe her, he could do so or whether he never saw beyond the familiar uniform of a staff nurse to the person beyond.

CHAPTER THREE

'CATHERINE, we're over here!' Catherine squinted across the dim interior of the crowded public bar of the Cat and Fiddle. Lizzie was standing in the open doorway of what appeared to be the pub garden. Behind her Catherine caught a glimpse of wooden, bench-type tables and brightly coloured parasols.

She'd gone home first to change so that she was ready to go on to the theatre after her drink. Fighting her way through the crowd around the bar, she joined Lizzie outside. At that elusive point where afternoon meets evening, it was still warm and the garden was bathed in sunshine. Children ran around between the tables and played on the swings in the far corner of the garden, while a quick glance revealed that every table was taken and that the garden of the Cat and Fiddle appeared every bit as popular as the interior.

'We've got a table,' said Lizzie. 'Simon got here first and he bagged one and spread himself around a bit to reserve a few chairs.'

'Simon?' said Catherine quickly. 'Simon Andrews? Is he here?'

'You bet.' Lizzie grinned. 'When he knew you were coming there was no holding him. Scott is here, so you'll meet him as well, and a few of the others have joined us.'

When they reached the table it was to find that quite a crowd of staff from the hospital was congregated there and Catherine guessed that this was a favourite

35

unwinding place. Together with Simon Andrews and a young man with closely cropped hair, whom she presumed to be Lizzie's live-in boyfriend Scott, there was also Lauren Keating, a staff nurse from their unit, Maggie Farman, an SHO, and another man whom Catherine couldn't remember having seen before. Simon had apparently been looking out for her because he leapt to his feet as she and Lizzie approached the table.

'Catherine,' he said. 'Nice to see you, glad you could join us. Do you know everyone?' He glanced round helplessly at the others as if when it came to introductions he didn't really know where to start.

'No, she doesn't,' said Lizzie, coming to his rescue. 'Catherine, this is my partner, Scott—he's a paramedic.'

'Hi, Cathy—nice to meet you.' Scott grinned and nodded.

'And this is Julian Farnbank,' Lizzie indicated the other man. 'Julian is a charge nurse on A and E.'

'Hello, Catherine.' Julian smiled.

'The rest,' said Lizzie, 'I think you know.'

'What are you drinking?' asked Simon. 'This is my round.'

Catherine glanced at the others and saw that they all had glasses. 'Oh, a spritzer, I think, please,' she said. 'A white wine spritzer.'

'Sit here,' said Simon indicating his place. 'I'll grab myself a chair on the way back.'

As Simon made his way across the garden and back into the bar Catherine sat down, thankful to take the weight off her feet after a busy day on the ward.

'He's been like a cat on hot bricks,' said Lizzie with a grin. 'He didn't think you'd come.'

As everyone looked at her Catherine felt her cheeks flush. 'I hope you told him I can't stay long,' she replied, trying to keep her voice light.

'On to another heavy date?' asked Maggie. Maggie was Canadian and had retained a very strong accent.

'Not really.' Catherine smiled. 'On to the theatre actually—and not the operating variety either.'

'Catherine is involved in amateur dramatics,' explained Lizzie. 'And, yes, before any of you ask I have warned Simon that she won't be staying for long.'

'Do you belong to LADS?' asked Julian with sudden interest, and when Catherine nodded he said, 'I'm also a member. But I'm not in this current production.'

'Me neither,' said Catherine. 'I'm helping out backstage this time.'

'Catherine has played some lead roles,' said Lizzie proudly.

'Really? What have you played?' Julian was obviously very interested and he and Catherine were still discussing different productions they had each taken part in when Simon returned with Catherine's drink.

The theatre talk continued for some time then gradually drifted into other topics before settling on shop talk and hospital management policies.

'We really are a right bunch,' said Lizzie at last. 'We can't wait to get away from work so that we can relax, then what happens when we get over here? All we do is talk about the hospital.'

'Have you seen Mr Grantham's tan?' asked Lauren Keating. 'Where does he go, for heaven's sake?'

Catherine found herself tensing at mention of Paul Grantham's name then listening hard for any answers or follow-ups. If anyone had asked her why, she couldn't have said. Really, she had no idea why she should be interested.

'I reckon he slips off to the Bahamas,' said Maggie with a sigh.

'No.' Lizzie shook her head. 'He has a villa in Spain.'

'And how do you know that? Paul Grantham's not the most forthcoming of men,' said Maggie. 'In fact, I would go so far as to say he's the most private man I know.'

'His registrar, Keith Prowse, told me,' admitted Lizzie. 'I'm certainly not privy to any of the great man's secrets.'

Suddenly Catherine had an almost uncontrollable urge to ask if anyone knew *anything* about him, like whether or not he was married, but she didn't quite dare.

The time passed quickly, and as the shadows began to lengthen Catherine glanced at her watch then drained her glass and stood up.

'Oh,' said Simon. 'You don't have to go already?' The look of disappointment on his face was quite comical and Catherine smiled.

'Sorry,' she said, 'but I do. Thanks for asking me.'

'Hope you'll join us again,' said Maggie. 'There are usually some of us over here most evenings.'

'OK,' said Catherine. 'I'll take you up on that.'

'I'll walk you to your car.' Simon rose swiftly to his feet, joining Catherine as she walked back into the pub.

'It's a shame you have to go so soon,' he said as they crossed the pub car park to her car. He paused. 'What time do you finish at the theatre?'

'Usually around ten o clock, but—'

'Perhaps we could meet then?' he asked eagerly. 'Maybe a bite to eat somewhere?'

'I don't think so.' Catherine shook her head. 'Thanks anyway but after a day on the ward and then a stint at the theatre, I'm usually dead on my feet.'

'Fair enough.' He shrugged. 'How about another evening when you don't have to go to the theatre?'

'Yes, all right,' Catherine heard herself say. 'I'd like that.'

'I'll catch you on the ward,' he said as she climbed into her car and he closed the door for her.

As she drove out of the car park he raised his hand in farewell. He really was rather nice, Catherine thought, in spite of Lizzie's stories about his chat-up lines. She still wasn't sure she wanted a relationship, though. It had been some time since the last one. That had been with Greg Travers, an SHO in the Oxford hospital where they had both been working. It had been a pleasant enough relationship but both of them had known that it hadn't really been going anywhere. It had finally fizzled out completely but they had parted on friendly terms and still exchanged cards and the odd telephone call. And, really, there hadn't been anyone since, at least no one serious.

Maybe all that was about to change. Simon Andrews was certainly the type she went for, with his dark hair and eyes and humorous, easygoing manner. And surely there wasn't any reason why she shouldn't enjoy a few dates with him without committing herself to anything heavy. And then, if things progressed from there, fair enough.

So, if that was the case, what was this niggle at the back of her mind? She frowned as she negotiated the traffic roundabout outside the park. It wasn't even anything she could put her finger on because it was so fleeting that it was gone before she could even give it shape or form, like an elusive dream that vanished on waking. She only knew it was something like a longing deep inside her that urged caution where forming relationships was concerned. She had been aware of it for some time now. It was as if she was waiting for something or someone who would fulfill that longing and somehow, since returning to Langbury, that feeling had intensified.

Could Simon be the one? She didn't know, but somehow she had her doubts.

She tried to put these disturbing thoughts out of her mind as she entered the theatre. She had a job to do and it was going to require every ounce of her concentration.

Abbie was on time and together she and Catherine took themselves off to a corner of the stage where Catherine sat down at the piano and prepared to put the girl through a vocal warm-up.

'I don't usually do that,' Abbie admitted.

'You should,' said Catherine. 'It could be part of the trouble. Every singer needs to loosen up their voice before singing, otherwise too much strain is put on the vocal cords. Now, we'll go through some simple scales, and I want you to start thinking about your breathing and where the breath is actually coming from. The other important thing, of course, is practice. I hope you practise regularly at home.'

'Not really.' Abbie pulled a face. 'You see my father's not too happy about me doing this.'

'What, singing?' Catherine stared at her. The girl had a beautiful voice and was obviously talented. It seemed inconceivable that anyone should want to suppress that talent.

'He likes to hear me sing…' Abbie said slowly.

'I'm not surprised—' Catherine began.

'But he worries about my school work. I'm sure he thinks I'm going to give up my studies and run away to London to perform in the West End or even Broadway…' Abbie's eyes were shining as she spoke.

'Which, of course, you won't do, will you?' said Catherine firmly.

'Well, I wouldn't mind going to drama school,' Abbie replied slowly.

'Most drama schools like you to have your A-levels first.'

'Yes, I know.' Abbie pulled a face.

'So how would your dad feel about that? If you passed your exams then were accepted by a reputable drama school where you could take a degree in theatre studies?'

'He might agree to that,' said Abbie doubtfully. 'I don't know. He's very anti-theatre.'

'We'll have to make sure he comes to see you in this production—that might change his mind,' said Catherine with a smile. 'Now, let's have your song once again.' She turned the page of sheet music on the piano stand. 'After three…'

When they had finished the half-hour's tuition the official rehearsal started and Catherine joined Rod in the stalls. They worked hard throughout the rehearsal, with Catherine making suggestions to Rod and keeping notes on what they discussed and points of continuity.

After Abbie's big scene and her rendition of 'Who Will Buy?', Rod turned to Catherine. 'Well, I don't know what you've done,' he said, 'but that was much better.'

'She wasn't doing any sort of warm up,' Catherine explained, 'neither was she breathing correctly. I've also emphasied the importance of daily practice if she wants to do any sort of public performance.'

'My word, you really are going to be an asset to this company,' said Rod. 'You wouldn't care to take on any of the others, I suppose?'

'I'll do what I can to help,' said Catherine, 'just as long as it's understood that I don't have any formal teaching qualifications.'

'Maybe not,' said Rod darkly, 'but you know a hell of a lot more than most people around here.'

'Abbie was telling me that her father isn't too happy about her performing.'

'I know.' Rod sighed. 'We never seem to get things quite right. It's all or nothing where parents are concerned.'

'How do you mean?' Catherine frowned.

'Well, they're either very pushy and wanting their offspring to play the lead when it's quite obvious the child in question simply isn't ready for it, or they disapprove of the whole thing and it's an ongoing battle to get them to agree to allow their child to perform.'

'Has it been that bad in Abbie's case?'

'Well, I had to speak to her father at the beginning because she came for the audition without his knowledge. He was none too happy when she got the part. Worried about her school work, I think.'

'But there are plenty of other youngsters who perform in these productions and they manage all right.'

'Yes, presumably, although in Abbie's case she attends that posh girls' school over at Middle Hampton.

I'm just afraid her father will throw a wobbly and make her pull out about half an hour before we open.'

'Would it help if I had a word with him?'

'It might, I suppose.' Rod shrugged. 'Maybe you could convince him that his daughter has real talent and that you're giving her some extra help...'

'How could I get to see him?'

'Not sure.' Rod hesitated. 'Although, come to think of it, I believe he picks Abbie up from rehearsals.'

'All right, leave it with me.' Catherine closed her notebook. 'I'll see what I can do.' There was a good chance that Abbie hadn't left the theatre yet and that her father hadn't picked her up. If she was quick she might just catch them.

The cast was pouring from the stage door following the end of rehearsal, spilling out into the large car park. It was almost dark now and Catherine paused on the steps, looking round for Abbie. She caught sight of her at last on the far side of the car park, the girl's pale blonde hair shining in the light from an overhead lamp as she appeared to be stowing her holdall in the boot of a car.

Quickly Catherine sprinted across the car park. She wasn't sure what she was going to say to the girl's father, but she had a vague idea that if perhaps she could persuade him to attend one of the rehearsals so that he could see what his daughter was doing it might help to alter his frame of mind over her taking part.

By the time Catherine reached the car she was slightly out of breath and the girl was about to climb into the passenger seat.

'Abbie!' she called.

The girl looked up. 'Catherine...is there anything wrong?'

'No. I just wondered if I could have a word with...' Catherine glanced at the driver's side of the car but in the half-light couldn't see who was sitting there.

Abbie looked bewildered for a moment then before anything else could be said the driver wound down his window, and in the slightly eerie light Catherine found herself staring down at Paul Grantham.

It was such a shock that she was rendered totally speechless while he didn't, by so much as the flicker of an eyelash, give the slightest indication that he had ever set eyes on her before.

'Oh...' she floundered at last. 'Mr Grantham...it's you! I didn't know...'

'Do you two know each other?' demanded Abbie across the bonnet of the car which now registered in Catherine's brain as being a Jaguar—a dark grey, very expensive-looking Jaguar.

It was left to Catherine to answer because Paul Grantham remained silent, his hands resting lightly on the car's steering-wheel as he averted his gaze from Catherine and stared straight ahead through the wind-screen.

'We work together...or, at least—' hastily Catherine tried to rectify that statement '—we both work at the same hospital, in the same unit.'

'I didn't know!' Abbie sounded incredulous. 'Are you a doctor?'

'Er, no, a staff nurse,' replied Catherine.

'This is Catherine, Dad.' Abbie leaned down in order to speak to her father. 'Remember I told you all about her, about how she's been helping me.'

'How could I forget?' Paul Grantham turned his head towards Catherine again and raised one eyebrow, the gesture somehow sardonic.

Catherine swallowed.

'What did you want to speak to me about?' asked Abbie curiously.

'Actually, I think it could wait.' Catherine took a deep breath in order to steady her nerves.

'In that case, Abbie,' said her father, 'we really should be getting along. We have to pick up Theo from the station.'

She couldn't have said more in any case because she'd quite forgotten what it was she had been about to say. Instead she took a step backwards as Abbie climbed into the Jaguar and shut her door and her father started the engine.

'I'll see you next time,' said Abbie, leaning forward so that she could see Catherine.

'Yes, all right. Bye, Abbie…'

'Bye, Catherine.'

Paul Grantham briefly inclined his head in her direction and then they were gone, father and daughter, purring out of the car park in the expensive grey Jag, leaving Catherine to walk slowly to her own car.

She sat for a long time, very still, as she absorbed what she had just learnt. It had been a tremendous surprise to find that Paul Grantham was Abbie's father and yet…and yet…on the other hand, in that split second when she had realised they were father and daughter, something had clicked into place in Catherine's mind. At first she hadn't even been aware what it was, but now, as she thought about it, she knew that it explained what she had seen before in Paul Grantham's eyes and had failed to recognise—and that had been his daughter's resemblance to him. The colouring was different, but the family likeness was striking.

So, now that she had established that fact, what was

this other feeling that was creeping over her? It felt suspiciously like despondency—but why should that be? What had changed in the last few minutes to make her feel this way?

She now knew for certain that Paul Grantham was married and had a daughter, but hadn't she assumed that anyway? Wasn't it inevitable that a man of his age, and an eminent consultant surgeon at that, would be married with a family?

Of course it was, she told herself firmly. She'd guessed as much anyway. But, reasoned a voice deep inside her, there was a vast difference in assuming something and actually having it confirmed. So, now that it had been confirmed, why was it bothering her?

She frowned and stared at the dashboard. It wasn't as if she had been attracted to him in any way. He was older than her for a start, not that that in itself was any sort of barrier, but he was her boss—head of the department in which she worked. In Catherine's experience at least, that *was* a barrier, and now, the biggest taboo of all—he was a married man.

She gave herself a little shake. What in the world was she thinking of, allowing her mind to travel along such lines? She would try and see if she could at some point have a word with the great man, but only where his daughter was concerned. Maybe it would be easier now that he knew who she was for her to convince him of his daughter's talent and persuade him to allow her to continue with her role in the show.

It was with that thought firmly uppermost in her mind that Catherine drove home to her cottage, so it was all the more disconcerting when that night her dreams were of a certain Mr Grantham.

They didn't start out that way. They began with her

and Simon Andrews singing a duet on stage, only for the scene to change to one of Catherine being chased through darkened hospital corridors. She didn't know who was chasing her, she only knew she was deeply afraid of her assailant—so much so that when a third person intercepted that assailant and rescued her from his unwanted attentions, she was so grateful that she ended up in her rescuer's arms.

He was taller than her and although not heavily built was surprisingly strong while his kiss, although demanding, was more tender than any she had ever known. The kiss led to love-making—on a hospital bed, no less—and it was only during this that she knew her lover to be not Simon Andrews, as she had suspected it might, but no other than Paul Grantham.

He was exciting, intensely exciting as he aroused her to undreamt-of heights of passion before leaving her suspended on the very pinnacle of desire for what seemed like for ever before expertly tilting the axis of her world and sending her soaring, higher and higher…

She awoke bathed in sweat and lay for a long time with her heart pounding, staring into the darkness, believing the dream to have really happened and wondering how on earth she would be able to face him the next day at work.

But then, as slow reality set in, she was left with a deep sense of disappointment that it *had* only been a dream, and once again that longing was back deep inside her, that longing for the unknown which had assailed her ever since her return to Langbury.

Eventually she slept again, albeit fitfully, only to awake tired and unrefreshed. In the cold light of day her dream seemed faintly ridiculous, and as she reached the hospital and walked into Gynae she was only too glad to put it right out of her mind and concentrate on the day ahead.

But, as with the best of all intentions, her plan immediately went awry for the first person she set eyes on as he walked out of Sister's office was Paul Grantham.

Because her dream was still so recent and because at the time it had seemed so real, her heart leapt in her chest as her gaze met his. For one delicious moment she allowed her eyes to linger on his lips as she recalled the private fantasy and then, as he spoke, the moment fragmented into a thousand pieces.

'Staff Nurse Slade.' His beautifully modulated voice was under the tightest control.

'Yes, Mr Grantham?' Catherine was surprised he even knew her name, but as she answered, the thought, crazy and impossible as it was, entered her head that maybe he, too, had experienced the same dream as her.

'I would like to see you in my office, please.'

Catherine felt her heart begin to pound. 'Of course. When...?'

'Now,' he replied abruptly.

CHAPTER FOUR

AFTER a brief word of explanation to a bemused Sister Marlow, Catherine followed Paul Grantham out of the ward and down the corridor to his office.

'This won't take long,' he said as she closed the door behind her.

'I assume it has something to do with Abbie.' Catherine took the chair he indicated while he moved round behind his desk. She knew if it had been about anything to do with her work it would have been pursued through different channels.

'You assume correctly.' He turned to face her but didn't sit down.

This morning the blue eyes appeared almost as grey as the sea on a stormy day and seemed to have lost their sparkle, leaving Catherine to wonder if all that charm really was reserved only for his patients. Briefly her mind flitted to her dream—he had been very different then—but quickly and firmly she dismissed the memory without giving it a chance to take hold. After all, it *had* only been a dream and it wouldn't do to let the memory of it lull her into a false sense of security.

'Actually,' she began, not giving him a chance to say anything further, 'I wanted to talk to you about Abbie...'

'Did you?' The tone was polite, the eyebrows raised, but his eyes were still bleak. 'Well, maybe this will save you the trouble because I want to know exactly what nonsense you've been filling my daughter's head with.'

'Nonsense?' Catherine stared at him.

'Yes, Miss Slade. That's what I said. Nonsense.' The gaze was level, the expression set.

Catherine took a deep breath. It was becoming pretty obvious that if she'd thought this man was going to be a pushover where his daughter was concerned she was going to have to think again. 'Mr Grantham,' she began, 'I can assure you that if your daughter's head has been filled with any nonsense, which I doubt because she seems a very sensible girl, it certainly hasn't been by me.'

'If that's the case,' he said smoothly, 'enlighten me. Was it or was it not you who suggested she could do a degree in theatre studies at a drama school?'

'Well, yes, yes, I did as a matter of fact...but...'

'Thank you, Miss Slade.' His eyes were like chips of blue ice now. 'You've just borne out what I said.'

'But that wasn't nonsense!' protested Catherine. 'That was just pointing out what was possible. Have you any idea how difficult it is to get into one of this country's top drama schools?'

'No,' he replied coolly. 'Neither do I wish to know.'

Catherine felt her hackles rise at his attitude. 'Maybe you would prefer your daughter to pack in her studies and just take off for London in the hopes of securing a part?'

'That's ridiculous. Of course that's not what I would want.'

'Well, then, I think you should—'

'But neither is there any danger of that,' he interrupted. 'Abigail has her schooling to complete and exams to take before she decides on her choice of university. We have already discussed the possibility of her pursuing a career in medicine.'

'And what about her acting and singing ability?' Catherine demanded coldly.

'What about it?'

'Is it simply to be ignored?'

He shrugged. 'Not necessarily, but neither do I want it overly encouraged. It should remain a pastime, a hobby.'

'But your daughter has talent, Mr Grantham—real talent—and a talent like hers should be encouraged.'

'I would say that is for me to decide. I can assure you I only have my daughter's best interests at heart.'

'In that case you will study her wishes,' declared Catherine hotly. Defiantly she faced him across the desk. The man was insufferable, for heaven's sake. How could she have thought that he was attractive? 'Have you for one minute even tried to take an interest?' she demanded. 'Do you know what part she has in this show? Have you heard her sing?'

'Of course I've heard her sing. She has a very pleasant singing voice—'

'Pleasant! Is that all you can say?' Catherine felt the colour flood her face. 'She has a beautiful voice! As yet it is untrained but—'

'I have heard her sing in her school choir...'

'Mr Grantham.' Catherine was holding onto her temper with difficulty now. 'May I suggest that you come along to one of the rehearsals so that you can hear for yourself just what Abbie can do.'

'That's another thing. These rehearsals are becoming very frequent and intrusive.'

'Rehearsals do tend to get that way in the build-up to an opening night.' She tried to keep the sarcasm from her voice. At this rate she was going to find herself out of a job. 'So will you come along one evening?'

'Won't the director object to that? I can't imagine he would want too many members of the public sitting in on rehearsals.'

'If it means Abbie being allowed to stay in the show I think he would agree to anything.'

Paul Grantham drew in a deep breath. 'I'll think about it,' he said, adding, 'Abbie says you have been giving her some tuition.'

'Hardly that,' Catherine retorted. 'I'm not qualified. Let's just say I've been giving her a bit of help.'

'I see.' He nodded. 'Well, Miss Slade, thank you for showing an interest in my daughter, but you now know how I feel about the situation.'

She was being dismissed and a moment later Catherine found herself outside in the corridor. She was still seething and it took quite an effort to bring herself under control as she strode angrily back onto the ward. Lizzie was standing at the desk in the nurses' station, checking through some records. She glanced up as Catherine approached.

'Hi,' she said. 'There you are. Glenda said Mr Grantham wanted to see you. Is everything all right?'

'Insufferable man!' said Catherine through gritted teeth.

'Who? Paul Grantham?' Lizzie looked bewildered. 'Why, what has he said to you? Was it about your work?'

'No.' Catherine shook her head, then in an attempt to pull herself together she said, 'You know I told you I've been helping a young girl with her part in *Oliver!*?

'Yes.' Lizzie frowned. 'What's that got to do with Paul Grantham?'

'Well, she only turns out to be his daughter.'

'You're joking!'

'I wish I was,' Catherine replied tightly.

'Did you know it was his daughter?'

'No, of course not.'

'You said that as if had you known you wouldn't have bothered.' Lizzie chuckled.

'Well, maybe I wouldn't,' Catherine replied darkly.

'So what's the problem?' Suddenly Lizzie sounded curious.

'He's very anti-theatre,' Catherine replied. 'Which sounds something of a paradox for a surgeon.' She paused. 'He can't seem to bear the thought of his daughter being involved in any way in the world of show business.'

'With all due respect, this *is* Langbury and amateur theatre we're talking about, isn't it?' Lizzie looked faintly incredulous. 'It's hardly Hollywood.'

'I know.' Catherine allowed herself a smile. 'But I think he's afraid of what it might lead to. It sounds as if Abbie would like to pursue the theatre as a career.'

'Could she? Does she have the talent?'

'Oh, yes, there's no doubt about that—with the right training, of course—but Daddy has other ideas. His plans for his daughter are very different. He sees her set for medical school. It even looks as if he might force her to pull out of the show.'

'I still don't see why he should have been having a go at you.'

'He thinks I've been encouraging her or, as he so charmingly put it, filling her head with nonsense.'

'Oh, boy!' Lizzie shook her head. 'Sounds as if he

could be heading for all sorts of trouble where his daughter is concerned. How old is she?'

'About fourteen, I would say—although it's hard to say. When she's on stage she looks older...'

'Can I expect any work out of you two today?'

Catherine had been about to say that she wondered whether it was any good approaching Abbie's mother over the problem but she trailed off as Sister Marlow came up behind them.

'Sorry,' she said instead. 'It's my fault. I've just been telling Lizzie about my summons.'

'Your summons?' Glenda Marlow frowned.

'Yes, to Mr Grantham's office.'

'Oh, yes. It wasn't anything to do with your work, I hope?'

Catherine shook her head. 'No, it was a personal matter.'

'Oh, I see. Not that I really thought Mr Grantham would ignore procedure. Anyway, now that you are here, we are running late. Helen Brooker is to go down to Theatre and Edna McBride is waiting for her bed bath.'

Vaguely relieved that Sister Marlow hadn't wanted to know what the personal matter was regarding herself and Paul Grantham, Catherine hurried onto the ward. She found Edna McBride sitting up in bed, reading a get-well card that had just arrived for her. 'That's better, Edna,' she said. 'You're looking more like yourself this morning.'

'That may be so,' Edna replied briskly, 'but I shall be pleased when I'm also *feeling* like myself.'

'You have to give yourself time,' said Catherine. 'Why, it's less than twenty-four hours since your operation. Now, tell me, have you been out of bed this morning?'

'Yes, I sat out while they made my bed.' Edna sounded faintly proud of her achievement.

'That's very good.' Catherine smiled. 'Eileen and I are going to give you a bed bath in a moment. Now, tell me, do you have any pain anywhere?'

'Not really...'

'Yes, she does.' It was Marion Finch who called out from the next bed. 'She just doesn't want to admit it. I told her she should tell you because if she doesn't you won't know, and if you don't know there isn't much you can do about it.'

'That's quite right,' agreed Catherine, while Edna pulled a face. 'So, Edna, I'll ask you again—are you in any pain?'

'Yes, I am, if you must know,' Edna replied crisply, 'but in my experience it doesn't do to complain.'

'I'll see that you get some additional pain relief,' said Catherine firmly. 'Actually, Edna, you're doing fine. You no longer have a drip and you're moving about very well.'

'I'll be glad when I get rid of this catheter,' said Edna, gritting her teeth.

'That may take a bit longer, given the nature of your operation.'

'I was afraid I was going to wet the bed all the time I had my catheter,' said Marion.

'Which is, of course, the one thing you won't do,' said Catherine.

'I know, but the trouble is you don't know when you want to go,' said Marion. Lowering her voice and indicating the bed in the far corner of the room where curtains were drawn around Helen Brooker, she added, 'Is she all right?'

'Yes.' Catherine nodded. 'She's resting before she goes down to Theatre. Now, tell me, Marion, are you going to have a go at getting down to the bathroom this morning or do you want another blanket bath?'

'Oh, I think I'd like to go down to the bathroom— if I can make it.'

'One of us will go with you,' Catherine explained, 'and if you don't feel able to get into the bath you can have a shower. I promise you, you'll feel so much better for it.'

By the time Catherine and Eileen had carried out Edna's blanket bath and had helped Marion to the bathroom it was almost time for the doctors' ward round.

Catherine found she was dreading seeing Paul Grantham again. She'd been angry when she'd left his office and he'd known it. But she'd had time to cool down a little since and was beginning to wonder if she hadn't overstepped the mark. He was, after all, the senior consultant on the gynae unit and he couldn't be used to one of the staff nurses speaking to him in such a way and certainly not about his own daughter.

The whole thing had just made her angry—his attitude towards the theatre in general, the fact that he'd thought that she'd been filling Abbie's head with nonsense and his casual, noncommittal approach to his daughter's talent. But in spite of all that she still had the uneasy feeling she might have gone a bit too far.

As she moved away from Edna's bed, after plumping up the pillows and making her comfortable, Catherine caught a sound from behind the closed curtains around Helen's bed. Opening the curtains a couple of inches, she peered inside and her suspicions were confirmed as she saw that Helen was crying. Quietly she slipped into the cubicle and closed the curtains behind her.

'Helen?' Gently Catherine touched the woman's shoulder. 'Is there anything I can get you?'

Helen started up then shook her head. Taking a clean tissue from a box on her locker, she wiped her eyes then blew her nose. 'I'm sorry,' she whispered. 'I can't help it. I just don't want them to have to grow up without me, that's all.'

'Helen, you musn't be—'

'Don't tell me not to be silly,' said Helen through her tears. 'I'm not a child, neither am I a fool. I've read a lot about my condition. Don't they call cancer of the ovaries the silent killer? I know the score.'

'Helen, you must try and remain positive,' said Catherine. 'There's a very good chance that this operation will be all that's needed.'

'If it hasn't spread, you mean?' said Helen wryly.

'There's a very good chance it hasn't,' said Catherine firmly, 'and that's what you have to cling to.'

'Yes, I know.' Helen dabbed her eyes again. 'And I also know I'm in the best possible hands. Mr Grantham said he will come and see me before my operation.'

'The doctors will be doing their round shortly,' said Catherine. 'After that we will be giving you your pre-med to help you to relax.'

'Do you think I could phone my husband before that?'

'Of course. I'll bring the phone trolley in for you.'

'I was hoping for somewhere a little more private.' Helen glanced at the closed curtains beyond which they could quite clearly hear Marion Finch's non-stop chatter as she regaled the long-suffering Edna with stories of her family.

'I'll ask Sister if you can use the phone in her office,' said Catherine quietly.

'Thank you. I think Colin will be feeling worse than I do this morning. And he's got the children to contend with...'

'Leave it with me.' Catherine opened the curtains then turned briefly back to Helen. 'The doctors have just arrived. I'll draw these curtains back for a while.'

'I hope my favourite surgeon is with them this morning,' said Marion as Catherine passed her bed.

'I'm sure he will be,' Catherine replied with a wry smile. It would be too much to hope that he wouldn't, she thought grimly.

Sure enough, Paul Grantham, as cool and immaculate as ever, was at the head of his entourage as they swept onto the ward. As Catherine would have tucked herself away, busying herself on the nurses' station, to her dismay Sister Marlow asked her to accompany the ward round.

If she had been aware of him before, she was doubly aware of him now after that episode in his office at the start of the day, but whereas before she'd doubted whether he even knew she existed, now she had the uncomfortable feeling that he was only too aware of her presence.

He was his usual charming self as the group stopped at Marion Finch's bed. 'I trust you're feeling a little better this morning, Mrs Finch.' He gazed down at her with a half-smile on his handsome features.

'Oh, yes, thank you, Mr Grantham,' she replied. 'Not quite the new woman you promised, but a little more human than yesterday.'

'Give it time, Mrs Finch. These things can't be rushed, but I'm a man of my word and, I promise you, very soon there will be no holding you and you will be living your life to the full again…in every respect.'

As Marion giggled Paul Grantham checked her observation chart and discussed a couple of the readings with Sister. 'The physiotherapist will be along to see you this morning to do some exercises,' he said as finally he replaced the chart on the bed rail.

'That sounds like hard work.' Marion pulled a face.

'Not at all,' Paul Grantham replied smoothly. 'Look on it as your contribution to this new woman we've been talking about.' With that he smiled at Marion then moved on to Edna McBride's bed.

It was only then that Catherine was suddenly aware that someone was watching her. Glancing up, she saw that Simon was part of that morning's team. Because she had been so wrapped up in what Paul Grantham might be thinking about her, she hadn't noticed Simon on the fringe of the group. While the consultant began talking to Edna and discussing her progress and treatment Simon stepped back from the others.

'Hi,' he murmured.

'Hi.' She smiled.

'I thought you were trying to avoid me.'

'No, of course not. Why should you think that?'

'I've been trying to catch your eye ever since I came onto the ward but all you seemed to do was to look the other way.'

'Sorry. It wasn't deliberate. I've got a few things on my mind this morning…'

'Dr Andrews,' a voice broke into their conversation, 'maybe you have an opinion on this?'

As Catherine trailed off she realised that Paul

Grantham was addressing Simon and that the rest of the group were looking at them, apparently waiting for some sort of reply.

'I'm sorry,' Paul Grantham went on smoothly, 'I hadn't realised you and Miss Slade were engaged in what appears to be a vitally important topic. If you would care to share the problem with us all I'm sure we can help you to solve it.'

'Er, no, I'm sorry, sir.' Simon flushed to the roots of his dark hair. 'It was nothing.'

'In that case can we all, please, bring our attention back to the case in hand?' Paul Grantham's gaze moved from Simon to Catherine then back to Simon again. It was the second time that day that he'd intimidated her and as she caught sight of Sister Marlow's icy stare, also for the second time that day, Catherine felt her anger rise.

He moved on to Helen Brooker, dismissing the rest of his group with the exception of Sister Marlow. Drawing up a chair, he sat beside Helen and proceeded to talk quietly to her.

Catherine made her way back to the nurses' station where Simon caught up with her. 'Sorry about that,' he said. 'I didn't mean to get you into trouble.'

'It's all right.' Catherine shrugged. 'I'm not exactly flavour of the month anyway where Mr Grantham is concerned.'

'Oh?' Simon looked puzzled.

'It's a long story,' said Catherine with a sigh. 'I'll tell you about it some time.'

'OK.' Simon nodded. 'How about tonight? Or do you have another one of those rehearsals?'

'No.' Catherine shook her head.

'In that case, how about a bite to eat in the Cat and Fiddle? Their food's pretty good.'

She hesitated, but only for a moment. What did she have to lose from a casual date with a colleague? 'All right,' she said, 'you're on.'

'Looking for something to do, Catherine?' Sister Marlow was behind them.

Simon pulled a face and moved away while Catherine shook her head. Suddenly she felt irritated with everyone. 'No, not really,' she said tightly. 'I promised Helen Brooker that I would ask you if she could use the phone in your office to speak to her husband.'

'What's wrong with the payphone?'

'I think she needs a little privacy.'

'Very well.' Glenda Marlow nodded.

'I'll organise that when Mr Grantham has finished talking to Helen,' Catherine went on. 'Afterwards I shall give her her pre-med. Until then I have a couple of admission forms to prepare.' Catherine spoke brusquely and for once Glenda had nothing to say.

By the time Paul Grantham returned to the desk Catherine was bent over her admission forms. Putting both hands palms downwards on the desk, he leaned forward. 'Thank you, Sister Marlow,' he called towards the office.

He was very close to Catherine, so close that one of his hands almost touched hers. Her first instinct was to withdraw her hand, but she didn't because the last thing she wanted was for him to think that the incident in his office that morning had in any way upset her. Instead, she remained perfectly still, not looking up once from the admission forms, her action, she hoped, implying that not only was she unfazed by what had hap-

pened between them but that she was completely un-
affected by, oblivious even to, his presence.

'Thank you, Mr Grantham.' Glenda came out of her
office and joined Catherine behind the desk.

'Mrs Brooker seems a little calmer,' he said. 'Apparently she's going to phone her husband before her
pre-med.'

'Staff Nurse Slade has that in hand,' Sister Marlow
replied.

'Very well.'

Still Catherine didn't look up, but she was never the
less aware that neither did Paul Grantham look at her.

Glenda Marlow took a deep breath and as the surgeon moved away from the desk to leave for the theatre
she said, 'Right, do what you have to do with Mrs
Brooker, Catherine, then I want a word—in my office,
please.'

With a sigh Catherine put her admission forms into
a folder and, leaving the desk, made her way to Helen
Brooker's bed. She was pleased to see that although
Helen's eyes were red she was no longer crying.
'Would you like to come with me, Helen?' she said.

Together they left the ward, aware as they did so of
speculation from Marion Finch.

'I didn't want to advertise the fact that you're using
the office phone,' said Catherine, 'otherwise they'll all
want to use it and Sister will have a fit.'

'This is kind of you,' said Helen, 'and I do appreciate it.'

The office was mercifully empty with no sign of
Glenda Marlow. 'Are you feeling a little better?' asked
Catherine as she stood back for Helen to precede her
into the room.

'Yes, a little,' Helen replied. 'Mr Grantham has had

a talk with me. He's wonderful, you know. He just seems to have that knack of inspiring so much hope.'

'Yes.' Catherine swallowed then, indicating the phone, said, 'There you are, it's all yours. I'll leave you to it. When you've finished go back to the ward and I'll come and give you your pre-med.' Taking a deep breath, she made her way back to the ward. She was beginning to wish she hadn't got up that morning. And the day was far from over—she still had Glenda Marlow to face.

CHAPTER FIVE

'RIGHT, what's going on?'

'What do you mean?' It was a little later and Catherine faced Sister Marlow across her office desk.

'Between you and Mr Grantham. I want to know what's going on.'

'There's nothing going on.'

'If there's nothing going on, how do you explain him wanting to see you in his office this morning?' Glenda Marlow's nostrils quivered slightly, a characteristic which her staff had come to recognise as a sign of trouble.

'I told you, that was a personal matter.'

'Yes, and I was prepared to accept that if that was where the matter ended, but that, apparently, isn't the case.'

'What do you mean?' Catherine stared at her.

'Well, Mr Grantham quite obviously reacted to your presence this morning at ward round when there seemed to be some antagonism over your dalliance with Dr Andrews, and then again just now in the nurses' station at the desk...'

'He ignored me at the desk,' Catherine protested.

'Exactly, and it was blatantly obvious he was ignoring you, just as it was obvious that you were going out of your way to ignore him. There was an atmosphere, Catherine, and I don't like atmospheres. So I'll ask you again what this matter is about between the two of you.'

'I told you—' Catherine could feel her exasperation rising '—it's a personal issue.'

'And that's fine until it affects the running of this ward and then it ceases to be personal.'

When Catherine stubbornly remained silent Glenda went on, 'Look, Catherine, I've been a ward sister for a long time and I think it's fair to say I've seen just about everything that could possibly happen between members of staff. I'll be perfectly honest with you. I don't like liaisons, affairs—call them what you like—between staff on my unit and especially when they are between my staff and senior consultants—'

'It's nothing like that!' Catherine stared aghast at Glenda. 'Surely you don't think that!'

'I don't know what to think! Mr Grantham asks to see you in his room. You are clearly upset afterwards and ever since there has been a decided atmosphere between the two of you.'

Catherine sighed. 'You're wrong,' she said. 'Quite wrong.' Taking a deep breath, she went on, 'Mr Grantham wanted to see me because of his daughter.'

'His daughter?' Glenda was clearly taken aback.

'Yes, his daughter Abbie goes to the same amateur theatre group as I do. Mr Grantham had got it into his head that I've been influencing her about choosing the theatre as a career.'

'And *have* you?' There was a decided note of indignation in the other woman's voice, as if the very idea would be a severe breach of hospital etiquette.

'Not really.' Catherine shrugged. 'She's a very talented girl and I'd simply pointed out a few possibilities, that's all. Those possibilities unfortunately didn't coincide with her father's plans for her.'

'Well.' Sister Marlow was obviously taken aback. 'So why didn't you say?'

Catherine shrugged. 'I didn't feel I had to.'

'So the two of you clashed over this?'

'You could say that.'

'I see.' Sister Marlow clearly didn't know quite what else to say. 'Well, I hope this isn't going to cause any further animosity. Like I say, I don't like anything that's going to jeopardise the smooth running of this unit.'

'There won't be any further trouble. Mr Grantham has made it quite clear where he stands over the issue. Likewise, he knows how I feel. As far as it goes, I should imagine the matter is closed.'

'And what about you and Dr Andrews?' Having exhausted one avenue, it seemed Sister Marlow was determined to find another.

'What about me and Dr Andrews?'

'Is that little issue going anywhere? Because from where I was standing, from the look on Dr Andrews, face it certainly looked as if it might.'

'I've no idea,' Catherine replied coolly.

'Very well. But a word of warning. Watch Dr Andrews. Yours wouldn't be the first heart he's broken on this unit.'

'I have no intention of allowing Dr Andrews to break my heart,' Catherine replied, 'or anyone else for that matter.'

'Good.' Glenda picked up a pile of folders from her desk. 'Now we have that sorted out we'd best get back to the ward. Helen Brooker will be ready to go down to Theatre.'

*　*　*

'Nosy old bag! Who the hell does she think she is, questioning you like that about your private life?'

It was much later and Catherine and Lizzie were at lunch in the hospital canteen. Catherine had just filled Lizzie in on her interview with Sister Marlow.

'She said she doesn't want anything interfering with the smooth running of the unit,' said Catherine, taking a sip of orange juice before unwrapping her pack of sandwiches.

'What she really meant was that she wanted all the gory details.'

'Only there weren't any. Honestly, me and Paul Grantham—can you imagine it? And then she even had the nerve to try to warn me off Simon—said he'd break my heart, or words to that effect.'

When Lizzie remained silent Catherine threw her a swift glance. 'Lizzie…?'

'Actually…' Lizzie said at last, wrinkling her nose.

'Oh, not you as well!'

'I have to say our Simon does have a bit of a reputation in that direction.'

'Well, he won't break my heart, I can assure you,' retorted Catherine.

'So who would it take to break your heart?' asked Lizzie lightly.

Catherine had been about to take a bite of her sandwich but she paused, disconcerted for a moment for, while considering Lizzie's question, an image of Paul Grantham had flashed into her mind. Not Paul Grantham as he had been that morning when he had been putting her in her place, or Paul Grantham the married family man, but the Paul Grantham of the dream she'd had the previous night. The sexy Paul Grantham who had made such passionate love to her,

who had been so tender, so exciting. Now, *that* Paul
Grantham could quite easily break her heart. But she
could hardly tell Lizzie that for there was no way her
friend would understand the dream or the effect it had
had on her.

Instead, calmly, she heard herself say, 'I'm not sure
really, but you needn't have any fears about Simon—
he's quite simply a friend and that's all.'

On their return to the ward they found that Helen
Brooker was back from Theatre and was being taken
care of by Lauren and Tiffany. Catherine was soon
caught up with two new admissions, dressing changes
and a medication round, while Lizzie disappeared into
the office with Sister Marlow to work out staff rotas.

It was almost at the end of her shift and Catherine
was at the nurses' station, preparing to go off duty,
when Paul Grantham suddenly appeared on the ward.
It was an unusual time of day for him to visit and
Catherine was struck by the fact that he looked tired.

'Can I help you?' she asked politely, only too aware
that at sight of him her heart had started to hammer
uncomfortably as she recalled their previous two en-
counters.

'Is Sister Marlow around?' He spoke quietly, the arrogance of earlier gone now, replaced by this more
reflective mood.

'She's in her office with Lizzie—Staff Nurse Rowe.'

'Thank you.' He nodded, came round the desk and
approached Sister's office, pausing with raised hand
before knocking and turning back to her. 'Perhaps
you'd care to come in as well,' he said.

'Me?' Catherine looked faintly alarmed.

'What I have to say concerns you all.' He knocked
and opened the door and Catherine followed him into

the office. What did he mean? Was this to be an official complaint? Her heart began to thump even harder and then, as Sister Marlow looked up from the desk and Lizzie frowned, her heart hardened. If he was about to make a complaint against her, she would give him a run for his money. Lifting her head, she tilted her chin, a gesture that, when she'd been a child, her father had said foretold trouble.

As Lizzie rose to her feet and would have left the room, Paul Grantham lifted one hand to detain her. 'Don't go,' he said. 'You all need to hear this. It's about Helen Brooker.'

'It isn't good news, is it?' said Sister Marlow.

'No, I'm afraid it isn't.' Paul Grantham shook his head and Catherine felt her heart sink. The personal anxiety she'd felt only seconds before seemed nothing now in the face of this very real human drama.

'I operated this morning, as you know,' he went on, 'performing a total hysterectomy. Unfortunately the cancer was already in the ovaries. We need to wait for the histology report and further scan results before we know whether it has spread elsewhere.'

'Should she be told immediately?' asked Glenda Marlow, even her usually brisk tone subdued now and tinged with compassion.

'I rather think not.' Paul Grantham stared at the desk. 'I'd like her to have a period of recuperation first then when she's a little stronger I'll talk to her and her husband together.'

'Can't anything else be done?' asked Catherine.

'We will offer follow-up treatment, of course,' he replied. 'It was extremely unfortunate that it had progressed so far before the initial smear was taken.'

'Had she had regular smear tests?' asked Lizzie.

'She admits she missed a couple,' he replied quietly.

Glenda Marlow sighed. 'If only people would understand how important routine screening is,' she said.

By the time her shift had ended Catherine was glad to get away. It had been a tough and difficult day in more ways than one, and it was with a feeling of relief that she drove home. Already she was beginning to regret having said she would meet Simon that evening for, if the truth be known, she would have liked nothing better than to kick off her shoes and put her feet up. Much as she tried not to let it happen, there were inevitably some cases that touched her more than others and Helen Brooker's was one of those.

While she showered and changed all she could think about was how she had found Helen crying because she didn't want her children to grow up without her. Then, even when she managed to put that image out of her mind, it was replaced by that of the look in Paul Grantham's eyes when he'd told them that the cancer had also been in Helen's ovaries.

After she'd fed Teazer she drove to the Cat and Fiddle. Simon had offered to pick her up but she'd told him she'd meet him at the pub. If he'd picked her up he would presumably have taken her home, and if that had been the case no doubt he would have expected her to ask him in. Maybe that's where it would end, she told herself, a cup of coffee, a chat, a brief goodnight kiss on the cheek. She'd be happy with that, but maybe he wouldn't. Maybe Simon would expect more. Given the gossip she'd heard about his reputation, it seemed there was a very good chance he *would* expect more.

Catherine still wasn't sure why she was so cautious about starting a new relationship, although deep down she felt it had something to do with this strange feeling she'd had since coming to Langbury. A feeling of waiting for someone, or for something that was about to happen, a feeling of being in limbo—and deep down some sixth sense told her this feeling had little or nothing to do with Simon Andrews.

He was already at the Cat and Fiddle, waiting for her, when she arrived. 'I've got us a table in the little dining room at the back,' he told her after he'd greeted her. 'That way we shouldn't be disturbed by any of the crowd if they turn up.'

She didn't have the heart to tell him that she wouldn't have minded if the others had joined them. She liked Lizzie's company and Scott seemed nice. Maggie was good fun and while Lauren was rather quiet Julian Farnbank was a sweetie and she could have gossiped for hours with him about the theatre.

Simon had been right about the food being good at the Cat and Fiddle, and Catherine found herself enjoying her meal. Simon was quick-witted with a keen, if sometimes slightly caustic sense of humour, but their conversation was centred mainly on himself. Catherine soon learnt about his family, his background in Sussex, his achievments and his ambitions.

'As far as I'm concerned, the sky's the limit,' he said. 'Registrar next, then consultant gynaecologist.'

'So Paul Grantham had better watch out.' She'd meant it as a joke but soon realised that Simon was deadly serious.

'There's no reason why I shouldn't achieve what he has,' he said. Then, his eyes narrowing slightly, he added, 'Talking of Paul Grantham, what was all that about this morning? You said you weren't flavour of the month where he was concerned.'

'No.' Catherine sighed then went on to explain to Simon about Abbie and the show. By the time she'd finished she felt that Simon had lost interest and in the end, after he'd gone on to tell her all about his skiing trips and the rugby team he'd played for when he'd been at medical school, she wasn't sorry when the meal was over. They walked out to the car park together.

'That was a lovely meal, Simon. Thank you,' she said as she unlocked her car.

'So is that it?' There was a quizzical smile on his handsome face as he looked down at her. 'Don't I get to come back to your place for a nightcap?'

'I'm sorry…'

'Or maybe you'd rather come back to my pad?' he went on, not giving her time to finish.

'No, Simon. I'm sorry, but I was about to say I'm tired—it's been a hell of a day and I'm ready for bed.'

'Well, yes.' He gave a slight shrug. 'Come to that, so am I…'

'No, Simon,' she said firmly.

'But it's early yet,' he protested, looking at his watch. 'Look, some of the others are only just arriving.'

'So they are.' Catherine looked across the car park to where Lauren, Tiffany and a couple of other members of staff whom she knew only by sight had just climbed out of a car. 'I'm sure they won't mind if you join them if you aren't ready to go home yet.' Reaching up, she gave him a light kiss on the cheek. 'Goodnight, Simon—and thanks again.'

He stood there, watching her, a look of bemused exasperation on his face as she drove out of the car park. He looked so dejected that for one moment she felt rather mean. Maybe she *should* have asked him back to her place. Then she dismissed the thought. If she had, it would have led to one thing. He had made that quite obvious by the way he had been looking at her during the evening. Catherine was no prude but she didn't like one-night stands and surely that's what this would have been had she let it, because deep down she knew she didn't want a long-term relationship with Simon.

Maybe, she thought, she shouldn't have gone out with him in the first place for it seemed casual friendship quite simply wasn't on Simon's agenda. But it irritated Catherine to think that if a man bought a meal he should assume it automatically entitled him to believe he could expect a night of passion in return.

By the time she reached her cottage she was feeling faintly depressed. Was it always going to be like this for her? There had been no serious relationship since Greg, and while this feeling of waiting for someone was all very well, if that someone didn't materialise, she could be in for a very lonely life.

Later, while she prepared for bed, she found herself trying to analyse what it was about Simon Andrews, and Greg Travers come to that, that had stopped her from wanting to pursue the relationships any further.

Greg had been very immature—she'd realised that as time had gone on—and a strong degree of selfishness had been bound up in that immaturity. Simon was very full of himself, as if the world revolved around him and his plans—once again, shades of selfishness and immaturity.

Maybe what she needed was someone older, she told herself, someone experienced not only in relationships but in the ways of the world. Someone who knew how to treat a woman.

Someone like Paul Grantham.

Unbidden the thought was there in her head, only to be dismissed immediately. Paul Grantham might be mature and experienced but there was also an arrogance about him which had been only too in evidence that very day when he had put her in her place. Would she want someone like that?

Of course not, she told herself firmly. And besides, Paul Grantham was married.

The next rehearsal for *Oliver!* was the following weekend, on Sunday afternoon. When Catherine met Abbie for her half-hour's tuition they found it difficult to find anywhere to practise as the stage was being used by the choreographer as he put the dancers through their various routines. They ended up in a corner of the ladies' dressing room, which was far from satisfactory.

'We'll have to try and find somewhere else in future,' said Catherine. 'It's impossible to practise without a piano.'

'We have a piano at home,' said Abbie.

'I can't see your father agreeing to let us practise there,' replied Catherine with a grimace.

'He might,' said Abbie. She hesitated. 'He told me he'd spoken to you, Catherine.'

'Did he?' Catherine felt herself tense, wondering quite what he'd told his daughter about that fateful encounter.

'Yes.' Abbie nodded, then earnestly she said, 'I don't know what you said to him, but he's been a lot better about things since then.'

Catherine stared at Abbie and once again was taken by the girl's resemblance to her father. 'You amaze me,' she said at last. 'He didn't seem very keen at the time.' She chose her words with care, not wanting to

disillusion Abbie by telling her that her father had accused her of filling his daughter's head with nonsense.
'So what has he said?' she asked curiously.

'Not a great deal,' Abbie admitted, 'but at least he's
agreed to let me stay in *Oliver!* and I think I've almost
persuaded him to come and see the show.'

'Well, that's wonderful.' Catherine smiled. 'I wonder what made him change his mind.'

'I don't know.' Abbie shook her head. 'I thought it
must have been something you said.'

'Well, maybe it was,' Catherine agreed with a rueful
smile. 'Maybe he took notice of the fact that I said you
have real talent.'

'You told him that?' Abbie's eyes widened and
when Catherine nodded she added breathlessly, 'Do
you think he might come round to the idea of drama
school?'

'Whoa!' Catherine held up her hands. 'I think you
need to take one step at a time.'

'Yes…I suppose…' Abbie wrinkled her nose.

'I wouldn't think you could rush your father over
anything like that but what about your mother—what
would she think about you going to drama school?'

'Oh, she'd probably be all for it,' said Abbie.

'Well, maybe you need to get her to talk to your
father,' said Catherine. 'But for the time being we have
a show to get out. Let's go and tell Rod that there's no
danger now about you having to pull out. He'll be delighted.'

The rehearsal went well, with Abbie apparently going from strength to strength. 'At this rate,' said Rod
after they had finished and everyone was packing up
and leaving the theatre, 'she'll soon be playing leads.
However did you manage to win her father round?'

'Goodness knows,' Catherine replied. 'I didn't think I had. In fact, I thought I'd simply made matters worse.'

'You must have made some impression if he's agreed to let her stay in the show.'

By the time Catherine left Rod most people had left the theatre, but as she passed the ladies' dressing room one of the dancers, a girl called Julie Gaskil, came out. 'Have you seen Abbie?' she asked when she caught sight of Catherine.

Catherine shook her head. 'I think she's gone.'

'She's left her bag behind,' said Julie. 'It's got her purse and everything in it. I would have taken it over to her house for her but I have to go to visit my parents in Oxford.'

'Where does she live?' asked Catherine. As she spoke she realised that she had no idea where the Granthams lived.

'Just outside Woodstock,' Julie replied. 'Look, the address is here on her purse.'

'Well, I'm going in that direction,' said Catherine slowly. 'I suppose I could go that bit further.'

'Oh, that's great,' said Julie, thrusting the bag into her hands. 'She'll be frantic when she discovers she's left it behind and they'll be locking this place up in a little while so even if she came back she wouldn't be able to get in.'

'Do you know if her father picked her up?'

'She said something about meeting her brother.'

'Her brother?' Catherine hadn't known Abbie had a brother, or for that matter, that Paul Grantham had a son.

'Yes. I think she said his name was Theo.'

'Oh, yes.' She remembered then. When she'd spoken

to Paul Grantham the night he'd picked Abbie up, he'd said something about picking someone called Theo up from the station.

'I must go or I'll be late,' said Julie. 'See you next time.'

'Yes. See you…' Catherine stood there with Abbie's bag in her hands as Julie dashed away down the corridor. Deep inside she was aware of some stirring of emotion, although she wasn't quite sure what it was. It was almost like a throb of excitement. But it couldn't be that. Surely not. After all, why should the prospect of going to Abbie Grantham's home to return her bag be the cause of excitement?

It was a sultry Sunday afternoon and the country lanes between Langbury and Woodstock were at the height of their summer glory. Tall cow parsley crowded the grass verges and the meadows on either side were thick with daisies, pink and white campion and great swathes of buttercups, while the road ahead shimmered in a haze of heat.

Catherine's spirits remained high as she drove but as she neared Woodstock a decided edge of nervousness crept in. This was Paul Grantham's home she was going to. Heaven knows what he would think about being disturbed on a Sunday afternoon, and by a member of staff at that.

Maybe he won't be there, she thought as she pulled into a layby and checked the address. Maybe his wife would answer the door. And suddenly curiosity took over as she tried to imagine what Paul Grantham's wife would be like. She had the feeling she would be beautiful, cool and elegant, while here she herself was in her old jeans and a baggy pink T-shirt, with little or no make-up and her hair slicked back behind her ears.

She found the address at last in a quiet, country lane with the name of the house, Ravenswood, inscribed on one of the black gateposts. The building itself wasn't visible from the road and Catherine hesitated for a moment before deciding to leave the car in the lane and approach the house on foot.

It was very quiet, the only sounds being that of bird-song and the distant hum of a plane. As Catherine began to walk her shoes made a loud, scrunching noise on the loose shingle of the drive, disturbing the peace of the summer afternoon. Bordered by thick banks of pink and blue hydrangeas, the drive curved first to the right then to the left, and the house, when it finally came into view, was a long, white building with leaded windows beneath a thatched roof. A large double garage was situated alongside the front entrance and one of its doors was slightly open, revealing part of the rear bumper of what looked like the dark grey Jaguar.

By the time Catherine reached the front door she was convinced that the entire household must have heard her approach, but everything remained silent and so still that not even a leaf stirred in the shrubbery. Taking a deep breath and with a hand that trembled slightly, she pulled the chain on the brass bell that hung alongside the door.

CHAPTER SIX

THERE was no reply and no sound from within the house. Catherine waited a couple of minutes then rang the bell again, and when all remained silent she walked slowly round to the side of the house. There was a wrought-iron gate set into the wall and cautiously she lifted the latch and pushed it open.

A crazy-paved pathway led to beautifully tended gardens. Deep herbaceous borders blazed with colour and in the centre of one of the neatly trimmed lawns a small waterfall tumbled over stones into a large pond, the sound both soothing and restful. On the far side of the lawns there was a tennis court and beyond that conifers and beech trees gave shade to what appeared to be a paddock. The scent from the many flowers and shrubs was almost overpowering, and for a long moment Catherine stood and absorbed the atmosphere.

Probably because she was so entranced she failed to see or hear anyone approach, so it made her jump when suddenly someone spoke at her elbow.

'Miss Slade. To what do we owe this honour?'

With an exclamation she turned sharply. Paul Grantham was standing behind her on the pathway. He must have followed her around the house.

'You startled me!' she said.

'I could say the same thing.' He eyed her up and down, no doubt taking in every aspect of her appearance, from the baggy pink T-shirt to her scraped-back hair. 'It's not every day I find a member of the nursing staff in my back garden.'

'I'm sorry,' said Catherine, 'but I did ring the bell. When no one answered I thought I'd see if there was anyone in the garden.'

He looked as cool and immaculate as ever in a pair of cream chinos and a navy blue shirt, while today those eyes looked as blue as the summer sky or the cornflowers in the flower-beds behind him. It made a change, however, to see him dressed casually and not in one of his habitual suits, or his white coat, or even theatre greens.

'I've brought Abbie's bag,' Catherine managed to say at last, holding out the green, rucksack-style bag. When he made no attempt to take it from her, she added, 'She left it at the theatre. Her purse is inside and we thought she might be worrying where she had left it.'

'We?' He raised his eyebrows.

'I'm sorry...?' Catherine was aware that her heart had started that uncomfortable thumping again, no doubt due to the fact that he had startled her. After all, what else could cause her heart to do such crazy things?

'You said ''we'',' he replied patiently. 'About Abbie's purse—you said, ''*we* thought she might be worrying where she had left it.'''

'Oh, yes—I meant Julie Gaskil and me. It was she who found the bag—she's one of the dancers in the show,' she added by way of explanation.

'Ah, yes—the show,' he said. 'So how did it go today?'

'Very well actually...at least the rehearsal did...' She trailed off. She'd been about to say that the practice beforehand hadn't gone so well, but she thought better of it. It probably wasn't a good idea to remind Paul Grantham of that. He, however, seemed to have other ideas.

'You said that as if there was some sort of problem,' he said.

'Not really…' She hesitated then decided to tell him anyway. 'It's just that we couldn't find anywhere for our…our practice.' She didn't really know what to call it, only too aware as she was of his disapproval over the whole issue.

'Oh? And why was that?'

'Well, previously we'd used the stage,' she explained, 'or at least one corner of the stage, but today the choreographer was using the stage to take the dancers through their routines and we were forced to go to the ladies' dressing room.'

'Which wasn't satisfactory?'

'No, not really.'

'Presumably because there were a lot of ladies dressing and undressing?'

'No.' She threw him a quick glance, for one moment thinking she detected a note of humour in his tone and that he was mocking her. 'It wasn't a dress rehearsal—we haven't got that far yet. It was because we didn't have any accompaniment. There's a piano on stage, you see.'

'Ah,' he said, 'I see. And you play the piano, Miss Slade?'

'Let's say I play enough to help Abbie with her scales and vocal warm-ups.'

'Fair enough.' He nodded and at last he took the rucksack from her. 'I'm not sure if Abbie is home yet,' he said. 'Her brother was meeting her from the theatre.

I've just walked into the village to post a letter and they hadn't got back before I left. But let's go and see.'

'Oh, it doesn't matter. I can just leave the bag…' Catherine began.

But Paul Grantham wasn't listening. Instead, he had moved past her on the pathway and was approaching a conservatory at the rear of the house. Taking a key from his pocket, he unlocked the door then indicated for her to join him. And suddenly, once again, she was curious. She wanted to see his home.

The conservatory was very large, with a mosaic-tiled floor, two overhead fans and cane furniture with deep cushions in shades of blue and terracotta. A low, tiled table in the centre of the floor was piled with glossy magazines and the Sunday papers. Plants lined the walls, some flowering in exotic colours, others with their green leaves polished until they shone. The conservatory led directly into what appeared to be an equally spacious sitting-room furnished with deep leather sofas and rich, dark furniture. On the far side of this room in a bay window stood a baby grand piano, its top covered with an array of silver-framed photographs of all shapes and sizes. Catherine would have liked to have lingered to inspect the photographs but Paul Grantham strode to the door.

'Abbie! Theo!' When there was no reply to his call he turned to Catherine with a slight shrug. 'I was right,' he said. 'They aren't home yet. They must have gone somewhere else first. Anyway, let me get you some refreshment. What would you like? Tea, coffee, a beer or some homemade lemonade…?'

'Oh, no, nothing, really…' she began hastily.

'I insist,' he said. 'It's the least I can do. It was good

of you to come all out here. It must have taken you out of your way.'

'Just a bit,' she admitted.

'So what's it to be?'

'The lemonade sounds nice.'

'It is.' He nodded. 'Come into the kitchen.' Not waiting for a reply, he led the way across the sitting-room, through a large, square hallway and into a dining-room which in turn led into a spacious kitchen.

Catherine was vaguely aware of a wooden block floor, fitted pine units and a dark blue Aga. Everything else was lost as she watched Paul Grantham take a jug of lemonade from the fridge.

'We always have plenty of lemonade on the go at this time of the year,' he said. Opening the door of one of the pine units, he took out two tall glasses in which he placed several cubes of ice before pouring the lemonade. Finally he took an orange from a large bowl of fruit, cut a couple of slices and placed one on the rim of each of the glasses.

There was a sense of unreality about the whole thing for Catherine couldn't quite believe where she was. She couldn't imagine what Lizzie would say the following day when she told her that not only had she visited Paul Grantham's home but that she had stood in his kitchen with him and watched him prepare drinks for them both.

'We'll take them into the conservatory,' he said.

Moments later she was sitting opposite him on one of the cane settees, the tiled table between them.

'So just how far out of your way did you have to go to get here?' he asked, taking a mouthful of his drink then placing the glass on the table. 'Do you live in Langbury?'

Catherine nodded, took a sip of the lemonade, which was delicious, and carefully set her own glass down. 'Yes, I live near the old priory on the Woodstock side of Langbury.'

'Even so, it was some way for you to come. How long have you lived near the priory?'

'I've only recently moved there.'

'I know you haven't been at the hospital for long.'

'I didn't think consultants noticed things like that.' She said it before she could stop herself.

'We probably notice much more than you give us credit for.' He paused. 'So where did you work before Langbury?'

'Oxford. I did my training there and have worked there ever since, but I must admit it's been nice to come back to Langbury.'

'Come back?' He raised his eyebrows. 'You came from Langbury originally?'

'Oh, yes, I was born and bred in Langbury.'

'So why the decision to return now? Do you still have family in Langbury?'

'Not really.' She shrugged. 'A few distant relatives, that's all. My mother died a few years ago.'

'And your father?'

'He and my mother were divorced. He's remarried and lives with his new family just outside London.'

'So where does that leave you?' His eyes narrowed slightly.

'Me? How do you mean?' She frowned.

'Do you have a family of your own? Are you married?'

'Heavens, no.'

'You said that as if marriage would be the last thing on your agenda.'

'No, not really. Not at all. Let's just say I've never yet met anyone I could visualise spending the rest of my life with.'

'I see.' He paused. 'Fair enough. But you still haven't said why the return to Langbury.'

'I'm not absolutely certain. Something drew me back—roots maybe. Familiarity—I don't know.'

'Maybe it was something telling you that this may be where you'll meet that someone with whom you would want to spend the rest of your life.'

It was such an unexpected comment for him to make that Catherine found herself staring at him in amazement. It also so accurately summed up her mood since returning to Langbury—the feeling of waiting and anticipation—that for a moment it left her reeling. Quickly she picked up her glass and took a gulp of the lemonade, then in a frantic attempt to change the subject she said, 'My return was probably influenced by the LADS being here as well.'

'The lads?' He frowned.

'Yes—the theatre group. Langbury Amateur Dramatic Society.'

'Ah, yes.' He nodded. 'I'd forgotten that's what they called themselves. So...' he paused '...are you saying you belonged to this group before?'

'Yes.' Catherine nodded. 'I was always a very active member. I love the theatre. I always have.'

'And do you have talent as well?' Once again Catherine thought he was mocking her, but when she threw him a quick, searching glance she found something rueful about his smile.

'I've been told so.' She replied briefly but was aware that as his attitude changed from being rueful to one of interest she felt the sudden colour flood her face.

'So are you in this production?' he said at last. '*Oliver Twist*, isn't it?'

'Not quite.' She felt a smile tug at her mouth. 'Just *Oliver!*, without the "Twist". And, no, I'm not in it. It had already been cast before I returned to Langbury.'

'And yet you're willing to help those who are in it, like my daughter?'

'Yes, of course. Why shouldn't I?'

'I'm sure that's very commendable of you, Miss Slade.'

'Not really. It's just doing something I love, and my name's Catherine by the way.'

He inclined his head slightly in acknowledgement then, leaning back in his chair, he surveyed her through half-closed eyes. 'I think,' he said at last just when she was beginning to feel uncomfortable, 'that I may owe you an apology.'

'An apology?' She guessed to what he was referring but didn't feel inclined to make it easy for him by letting him know she'd guessed.

'Yes.' He nodded. 'On reflection, I feel I may have been rather, shall we say, over-protective where Abbie is concerned? And I may have taken it out on you. But I assure you, I only have my daughter's best interests at heart.'

'I'm sure you have.'

'It isn't easy, bringing up teenagers in today's climate.'

'I can imagine.' Catherine nodded. 'But I don't think you need have any fears where Abbie is concerned. She seems very sensible and level-headed.'

'Oh, I don't doubt that. But she's also very determined and she knows exactly what she wants. I also realise, however, that the more I oppose what she wants the more likely she will be to rebel and do her own thing. I'm sure she will have told you that I've said I have no objection to her continuing with this production. It is, after all, summer and it shouldn't interfere with her schooling too much.'

'And any future productions?'

'Shall we just take one step at a time?' He raised one eyebrow.

'Maybe that would be a good idea.' Catherine smiled, suddenly and unexpectedly at ease with him.

They were silent for a moment then he asked, 'You said you believe she has real talent?'

'Yes, I do. She has a lovely voice and, of course, if she intends to take this any further she really will need professional tuition…'

'But in the meantime you and she need somewhere to practise?'

'Well, yes, like I say, if we're lucky we get to use a corner of the stage. If not…' She shrugged.

'Would it be helpful if you were to come here and practise?'

'Here?' Startled, Catherine allowed her gaze to meet his. It was what Abbie had mentioned but Catherine had never thought he would agree. Now, here he was, suggesting it himself.

'Yes, we have a piano. For the most part it's sitting here, doing nothing. Both the children were taught to play when they were younger, but now…' He shrugged dismissively. 'So, would it help?' he added.

'Well, yes. Yes, of course.'

'OK. Sort it out with Abbie.'

'But won't we disturb you?'

'I'll leave it to Abbie to make sure you don't coincide with when I have a clinic for my private patients.

Otherwise, it's no problem.' He looked up sharply as somewhere in the house a door clicked. 'Sounds like they're home,' he said rising to his feet.

Catherine half turned in her chair as Abbie erupted into the conservatory. 'Dad, you'll never guess what Theo said…' She trailed off as she caught sight of Catherine, her eyes widening in amazement. 'Catherine! Whatever are you doing here?'

It was her father who answered. 'Catherine has very kindly brought your bag, Abbie. You left it at the theatre.'

'Did I?' Abbie looked bewildered for a moment. 'Gosh, yes, I suppose I did. Oh, thanks, Catherine, that was really cool of you.'

'That's OK.' Catherine smiled but her glance flickered to the tall, good-looking boy who had followed Abbie into the conservatory. He looked about seventeen and, with the startling combination of dark hair that flopped across his forehead and bright blue eyes, he gave Catherine an insight to how his father must have looked at the same age.

'Catherine, this is my brother, Theo.' It was Abbie who rushed to carry out the introductions. 'Theo, this is Catherine.' Impulsively she turned to her brother. 'It's Catherine who's helping me with my singing.'

'Hello, Catherine.' The boy's smile was the same as his father's.

'Nice to meet you, Theo.'

'Abbie.' Paul Grantham turned to his daughter. 'Catherine has been telling me about your difficulty in finding somewhere to practise…'

'Yes,' Abbie agreed, 'it was horrendous today—'

'Well, we've decided that Catherine will come here and you can use the piano in the sitting-room.'

'Oh?' Abbie looked taken aback for a moment. 'That's cool, Dad,' she said. 'Thanks.'

A little silence followed which could have become uncomfortable if left to grow, so Catherine rose to her feet. 'I really must be going,' she said. 'Thanks for the lemonade. It was delicious.'

'I'll see you out,' said Abbie.

'Goodbye, Catherine.'

'Goodbye, Mr Grantham.'

She followed Abbie out of the conservatory, across the sitting room and into the hallway. This time she became aware that there was another room, off the hall, its walls lined with shelves of books, a computer sitting on a large desk. This, no doubt, was the study where Paul Grantham saw his private patients.

'Whatever did you say to make Dad offer to let us practise here?' murmured Abbie as she opened the front door.

'I only told him how difficult it had been at the theatre.'

'Well, whatever you said, it worked. I can hardly believe it, especially with the mood Dad's in at the moment.'

'You mean over you doing the show?' Catherine frowned.

'No—he's OK over that now.' Abbie's voice dropped to a whisper. 'I mean over Theo.'

'Theo?'

'Yes, he was suspended from school for "wild be-haviour". Dad was absolutely furious—but maybe I shouldn't have told you that.' Abbie glanced over her shoulder. 'Don't let on, will you?'

'Of course not. Now, Abbie, I really must go.'

'When will you come here?'

'Can I phone you after I've checked up on my shifts?'

'Yes, all right. Bye, Catherine, and thanks again for bringing my bag back.'

Abbie stood in the doorway as Catherine set off down the drive raising her hand in farewell as Catherine turned back once before reaching the first bend. A second car was parked in front of the garage now, a bright red Polo which Catherine assumed belonged to Theo.

It had been an enlightening half-hour in more ways than one, for where Paul Grantham's home and lifestyle had more than measured up to expectations, there were other areas of his life that seemed to have more than their fair share of problems. She had almost reached the end of the drive when an oncoming car suddenly forced her to step aside into the hydrangea bushes.

The car was dark blue and open-topped, either a BMW or a Mercedes, Catherine thought as it passed her. Because of its close proximity she was able to see the driver quite clearly. It was a woman, her blonde hair caught back from her face and fastened at the nape of her neck with a black bow. Much of her face was hidden behind sunglasses but Catherine had a glimpse of expensive gold jewellery, a silk scarf with a leopard-skin pattern and slim, tanned hands on the steering-wheel. The woman seemed not to have noticed Catherine as she passed or, if she had, she chose not to acknowledge the scruffy-looking figure squashed in ungainly fashion against the hydrangea bushes.

Well, at least, she'd been right about that, Catherine thought as she unlocked her battered little Renault and slipped behind the wheel. When she'd first met Paul

Grantham she'd imagined him with a cool, blonde trophy wife and that was precisely what she'd just seen
behind the wheel of the open-topped car.

She drove home to her cottage in a strange, almost
restless mood and for the rest of that day she found
she couldn't get the Grantham family out of her mind.
Their home had been just as she had imagined the
home of a successful consultant to be, and constantly
images of it filled her head—the long, white, thatched
building, the lovely gardens, the tennis court and the
paddock. She thought of Paul Grantham's children, the
talented and vivacious Abbie so determined to have her
way, and the handsome Theo in deep trouble with his
school. She thought of the glamorous-looking woman
in the open-topped car who had simply exuded wealth,
beauty and privilege, but most of all, to her dismay,
she found it was thoughts of Paul Grantham himself
that crowded her mind.

She had to stop this, she told herself angrily later
that evening. This man was married for heaven's sake,
he was out of reach—an untouchable, Lizzie had called
him. So if that was the case why couldn't she simply
switch off, transfer her thoughts onto something or
someone else?

Why not ring Simon and invite him over to her place
for a meal? He'd made his interest in her plain enough.
She could cook a special meal, play the right music,
light candles, create the right romantic atmosphere. But
then what? Simon wouldn't be content to leave it there,
she knew that. He would expect to stay the night. And
that was the last thing she wanted. But why? Simon
was a nice enough guy so was it just him she didn't
want to get close to or was it men in general?

But then her mind went off at a tangent. What if it

were Paul Grantham she was cooking a meal for? What if it were him she was creating the right atmosphere for? What if he were free, would she do it then? And the answer came back to her loud and clear that, yes, yes, of course, she would. Just the thought of it caused her pulse to race and her heart to beat faster. The thought of those eyes gazing into hers, those arms around her, those strong, surgeon's hands on her body.

She felt a shaft of excitement course through her. That was how it had been in the dream she'd had about him. That had seemed so real, almost as if it had really happened, as if he really had made love to her.

And that, when she thought about it, was quite ridiculous because there was no way that he would look at her, even if he were free. She quite simply wasn't in the same league as the type of woman he would go for, the type of woman like his wife, the type of woman who wore designer clothes, expensive jewellery and who drove a top of the range car.

Somehow she got through the rest of the evening, and on Monday morning she faced the prospect of going onto the ward and meeting Paul Grantham again with a heady mixture of fear and anticipation. Everything had changed somehow, because now she had a social contact with the consultant surgeon as well as a professional one.

CHAPTER SEVEN

'SUE O'NEILL was admitted last night for emergency surgery on an ovarian cyst.' Glenda Marlow glanced round at her staff who were assembled for morning report. 'Dr Prowse performed the surgery. Marion Finch is for discharge today, but in view of her age and the fact that she lives alone we've decided to keep Edna McBride for a further forty-eight hours.'

'What about Helen Brooker?' asked Lizzie.

'Mr Grantham is to speak to Helen and her husband later this morning after his outpatient clinic. We have two new admissions this morning for surgery tomorrow. One has pelvic inflammatory disease and the other is eleven weeks pregnant and has had a threatened miscarriage. Lizzie, perhaps you could take the PID case. Catherine...' She looked up, her gaze falling on Catherine. 'If you could admit the miscarriage. The others this morning are all purely routine.' She went on to list the other patients on the ward and the current stage of their treatment.

'Good weekend?' asked Lizzie a little later as they filed out of Sister's office onto the ward.

'Yes,' Catherine replied. 'And you?'

'We've been decorating.' Lizzie pulled a face. 'So if you can call that a good weekend then, yes, I suppose it was. What did you do?'

'You know, all the usual. Shopping, cleaning, oh, and we had another rehearsal yesterday afternoon.'

'How about you, Lauren?' Lizzie turned as Lauren came up behind them. 'Did you have a good weekend?'

'Some of us were on duty.' Lauren wrinkled her nose then, ignoring Catherine, she hurried off to the sluice room.

'Tell me,' said Catherine, staring after her, 'do you know if I've done anything to upset her? She's been really off with me practically since the moment I arrived on this unit.'

'I wouldn't say it was actually anything you've done,' said Lizzie, 'more simply a case of just being here.'

'Whatever do you mean?' Catherine stared at Lizzie.

'Well, our Lauren thought she was well in with a chance with Simon until you arrived on the scene. In fact, I think they even went out together a few times, but lately he doesn't seem to have noticed that she even exists because he can't take his eyes off you.'

'Oh, Lord!' Catherine looked aghast. 'So that's it. I knew there was something. Well, as far as I'm concerned, she can have him,' she said, hurriedly adding, 'Oh, don't get me wrong. He's a nice enough guy but I'm just not that interested.'

'I really thought that you and Simon might go places.' Lizzie eyed her shrewdly. 'What went wrong?'

'Don't know really.' Catherine shrugged.

'Not your type, or maybe…' Lizzie threw Catherine another sidelong glance '…there's someone else, someone you haven't told us about. Is that it?'

'I should be so lucky.' Catherine spoke lightly but for some obscure reason she felt the colour touch her cheeks and she knew Lizzie had seen it. On the pretext of getting on with the morning's work she got away from Lizzie and went onto the ward where she found

Marion Finch in a pink satin dressing-gown, sorting out
the contents of her locker in readiness for going home.

'Is your husband coming for you, Marion?' she
asked.

'Yes, bless him,' Marion replied. 'I've asked him to
bring my clothes. I just wonder what he'll bring. Last
time I was in hospital, when I had my D and C, he
brought my oldest clothes, the ones I wore for housework and gardening. He said that's what I always wore,
so that's what he thought I'd want. Honestly, I ask you.
Men!' Marion laughed then, turning back to her locker,
she said, 'Just look at this lot—you'd think I'd been
here for a month instead of just a week.'

Catherine watched for a moment as into a large holdall Marion packed toiletries, fruit, get-well cards, boxes
of sweets, notelets and tissues, and a bottle of orange
squash. 'I expect,' she said, 'you'll be glad to get home
now.'

'Yes, I will,' Marion replied. 'Oh, don't get me
wrong,' she added hastily. 'You've all been wonderful,
but I can't wait to sleep in my own bed again and it'll
be lovely to have my daughters and the grandchildren
popping in to see me.'

'There's no place like home,' said Catherine. 'But
you must remember not to overdo things to start with.
No housework or lifting, no stretching up, and make
sure you have a rest in the afternoons at least for the
first few weeks.'

'Sounds like heaven,' said Marion with a grin. 'I
can't wait. Sister says I can't phone my husband yet to
come and get me, not until I've seen Mr Grantham.'

'The doctors should be round shortly,' said
Catherine.

'Poor old Edna can't go today, can you, Edna?'

Marion turned to Edna McBride, who was sitting in the armchair beside her bed. 'Never mind, Edna, they'll probably let you go soon.'

Catherine moved round the bed. 'Hello, Edna.' She smiled. 'How are you feeling this morning?'

'Rather tired,' Edna replied.

'Does it worry you that you won't be going home today?'

'Not really. I may get some rest later.' Her glance flickered towards Marion but the irony was lost on the younger woman.

'I told Edna...' Marion looked up from her packing '...we'll have to visit each other when we're feeling better. I've given you my phone number, Edna, haven't I? Now, let me check that I have yours. I think it's important that you keep up with the people you meet in hospital—do you know, I still keep contact with a woman who was in the maternity ward with me when I had my eldest girl? Now, what do you think of that?'

Edna's gaze briefly met Catherine's. 'Tell me, Edna,' said Catherine, a smile hovering around her mouth, 'how will you manage when you get home?'

'I have arranged for a home help to come in,' Edna replied crisply. 'I didn't want to but Mr Grantham persuaded me it would be for the best. My sister is also coming in each day just to keep an eye on me.'

'Oh, here they come,' called Marion suddenly. 'I have to say this is the bit I'll really miss, all these dishy doctors coming to see me each morning—and one in particular.'

Somehow Catherine found it difficult to meet Paul Grantham's gaze. She'd found it difficult to look at him before, after he'd bawled her out, but this was different.

It had all changed now. He'd been kind to her, and the awareness was even more intense. The group of doctors went to Marion first and Paul Grantham took the folder from Sister Marlow and opened it.

'Ah, Mrs Finch,' he said as Marion sank down into the armchair beside her bed and gazed up at him, a rapt expression on her face. 'I believe you would like to go home today.' He scanned her notes. 'Well, I don't see any reason why you shouldn't. You've had your drain removed, and your clamps, and you're down to very mild pain relief now. Has the blood loss decreased?' He glanced at Sister who nodded.

'Yes,' she replied, 'it's negligible now.'

'Good. Blood pressure, pulse and temperature are normal. No signs of infection. So I would say you are well on the way to becoming that new woman I promised.' He smiled his dazzling smile and, in spite of herself, Catherine felt her heart turn over.

Stop it, she told herself desperately. He was untouchable. Forbidden. She mustn't feel this way.

The group of doctors moved on to Edna McBride and as Paul Grantham approached the spot where Catherine stood his gaze met hers. In the past if that had happened he would have simply looked away, or the most he would have done would have been to incline his head slightly in acknowledgement. This morning, however, he smiled. 'Good morning, Catherine,' he said softly. 'Are you well?'

'Good morning, Mr Grantham. Quite well, thank you,' she murmured. She knew that hated colour had touched her cheeks again and suddenly, desperate in case someone else may have noticed, she glanced surreptitiously at the other members of staff. Fortunately Simon wasn't there that morning, he would have noticed for sure, and Sister Marlow, who also might have noticed, had chosen that moment for a brief word with Marion Finch. But the one person who *had* noticed was Lizzie Rowe, and to Catherine's confusion she was staring at her with raised eyebrows and a look of amazement on her face.

Quickly Catherine looked away and tried to concentrate on what was being said to Edna.

If she'd thought she'd got away with it, however, she was wrong because later, after the doctors had gone, the new patients had been admitted and Derek Finch had come to collect his wife, Lizzie cornered her in the sluice.

'So what was all that about?' she demanded curiously.

'All what?' Catherine deliberately feigned innocence.

'With you and Mr Grantham during the doctors' round.'

'Me and Mr Grantham? I don't know what you're talking about.' She tried to push past but Lizzie was barring the door.

'Oh, yes, you do. Last week the pair of you were at loggerheads—"an insufferable man" was how you described him, if I remember rightly. And now here you are, simpering and blushing like a lovesick schoolgirl, while he's smiling, calling you by your Christian name and going out of his way to enquire after your health.'

'I was *not* simpering and blushing,' protested Catherine hotly.

'Yes, you were,' said Lizzie. 'Just like you are now.'

'I'm not...'

'What I want to know is what changed and when.

Come on, Catherine. I'm not stupid, I know something must have happened. Was it at that rehearsal of yours?'

Catherine maintained a stubborn silence but when Lizzie urged her once more to tell her what had happened she at last gave a shrug.

'Well, if you must know,' she admitted at last, 'it was after the rehearsal.'

'*After* the rehearsal? This is getting interesting.' Lizzie's eyes gleamed. 'Did he give you a lift home? Or did you go for a drink with him?'

'Of course not,' Catherine protested. 'It was nothing like that. His daughter Abbie had left her bag at the theatre. I was asked if I would take it home for her as the theatre was about to be locked up for the night.'

'So did you?' Lizzie was beginning to look more than interested now.

'Yes.' Catherine nodded.

'So you went to the house? Mr Grantham's house?' Lizzie's eyes widened. 'What was it like?' she demanded. 'I've heard it's fabulous.'

'Yes, it is,' Catherine agreed. 'It's a beautiful house—what you would expect for a man in his position.'

'Woodstock, isn't it?'

'Just outside, actually.'

'So go on, tell,' prompted Lizzie when Catherine fell silent.

'What do you want to know? There isn't really much to tell.'

'Well, for a start, was he there? Were you asked in?'

'When I got there no one was in, then he—Mr Grantham—came home and he asked me in.'

'Go on.' Lizzie was agog now. 'What happened next?'

'He insisted I have a drink—'

'What did you have?'

'Lemonade actually.'

'*Lemonade!*' Lizzie looked incredulous. 'Oh, that's just typical of someone on a consultant's salary. Didn't he have anything stronger than that, for heaven's sake?'

'Actually, it was delicious.' Catherine found herself defending him. 'It was home-made and ice cold. If you remember, Sunday was very hot—and this *was* the middle of the afternoon!'

'So what was he like towards you?' Lizzie quite obviously wasn't going to let the matter drop there.

'He was OK...'

'Bearing in mind he'd previously had a go at you for filling his daughter's head with nonsense.'

'Yes, I know, but somewhere along the line he must have had a change of heart because he'd already told Abbie that she could stay in the show. There'd been fears that he was going to make her pull out,' she explained when she saw Lizzie's puzzled look. 'Anyway, he must have mellowed over the whole thing because he's even said we can practise at their house and use the piano there.'

'What!' Lizzie's jaw dropped.

'It's no big deal, Lizzie...' Catherine trailed off as Sister Marlow suddenly appeared at the door of the sluice room.

'What *is* going on in here?' she demanded. 'Look, if you two can't find any work to do—'

'It's all right,' said Catherine quickly, 'we're going.' For once she was glad for Glenda Marlow's interruption because the conversation with Lizzie seemed to be getting out of control. Not looking at Lizzie again she hurried back onto the ward and to the bedside of the patient she had recently admitted.

Lisa Wallace was twenty years old, recently married and expecting her first baby. She was also very frightened. While admitting her, Catherine had learnt that she'd suffered a threatened miscarriage at eight weeks and this latest scare at eleven weeks. She was now resting quietly in bed but she was very tearful.

'Try and relax, Lisa,' said Catherine.

'I can't,' whispered the girl. 'I don't want to lose my baby...' Tears flowed freely down her cheeks and Catherine took a couple of tissues from an open box on the locker and handed them to her.

'Come on,' she said gently, 'dry your eyes. Your baby may be perfectly all right. That's why you are here, so that we can make sure that everything is going according to plan.'

'When's the doctor coming? I want to see the doctor.' There was an edge of panic in the girl's voice.

'He'll be along shortly,' said Catherine.

'Can *I* help?'

Catherine had been leaning over Lisa's bed but she turned at the sound of a voice and saw that Helen Brooker was on her way back from the bathroom to her own bed.

'This is Lisa,' said Catherine. 'She's a bit unhappy at the moment.'

'Hello, Lisa.' Helen made her way slowly to the chair beside Lisa's bed and very carefully lowered herself into it. 'Just had a little op.' She pulled a face and Lisa turned to look at her. 'I heard them say you have a threatened miscarriage?'

Lisa's eyes filled with fresh tears and she nodded.

'I had one of those once,' Helen said.

'And was everything all right?' Lisa threw her a fearful glance.

Catherine took a deep breath, poised to intervene, knowing that Helen Brooker had told her that she'd once suffered a miscarriage but before she had the chance to say anything, Helen spoke again.

'Well,' she said in a matter-of-fact tone, 'my Joe's a strapping ten-year-old now and I went on to have two more after he was born.'

'Did you?' Lisa dried her eyes and Catherine bit back what she had been about to say. It was obvious that Helen had assessed the situation and was responding accordingly.

'Shall I sit with you for a while?' asked Helen.

'Yes, please,' said Lisa.

'Is that all right, Nurse?' Helen's gaze met Catherine's.

'Yes, just for a while.' Catherine nodded. 'But don't tire yourself, Helen. I'll be back in a while. I have to check your wound and change your dressing pad.'

'The doctor's coming to see me soon, isn't he, Nurse?' Lisa looked from Helen to Catherine.

'Yes,' Catherine agreed. 'He'll be along shortly.'

'He's coming to talk to me as well,' said Helen. 'Isn't that right, Nurse?'

'Yes, I believe he is.' Catherine nodded. Leaving the two women talking together, she moved on to the second new admission of the day. Helen Brooker didn't yet know that her husband was on his way to the hospital so that Paul Grantham could speak to them both together.

The other patient to be admitted that morning was Maria Elliott, a young woman in her twenties who was suffering from chlamydial infection and recurrent episodes of pelvic inflammatory disease. She had been given pethidine on admittance as an analgesic to control her pain and was resting quietly.

Catherine checked Maria's pulse and blood pressure and noted from her care plan that, following blood tests, it had been decided to allow her to rest for a while before undergoing any further examinations.

'I want to see my boyfriend,' Maria muttered sleepily as Catherine checked and adjusted the intravenous infusion that had been set up following her admission.

'I expect he'll be in to see you at visiting time.'

'I want to see him now.'

'You have to rest now,' said Catherine firmly. 'Rest is very important with your condition.'

The girl sniffed and turned her face to the wall.

The busy ward routine continued and to Catherine's relief there was no other opportunity for Lizzie to question her further, although she knew that her friend wouldn't be content to leave things at that.

And then just before the patients' lunchtime Paul Grantham and Simon Andrews arrived on the ward following their outpatient clinic.

Sister Marlow was in a meeting, Lizzie was occupied with the patient who'd had an ovarian cyst removed and Lauren was in the office, completing paperwork, so it was left to Catherine to accompany the two doctors. They went to Lisa Wallace first.

'Lisa.' Paul Grantham took her hand. 'When I told you in Antenatal that I'd see you soon, I didn't mean this soon.'

'I know,' whispered Lisa. 'Oh, Mr Grantham, everything will be all right, won't it?'

'I don't see why not,' he replied. 'But to be on the safe side I think I'd better just check to make sure baby is behaving. Nurse Slade?' He glanced at Catherine who nodded and drew the curtains.

'I'll go and have a word with Miss McBride.' Simon moved away, leaving Catherine to slip back into the cubicle. Carefully, while Paul Grantham donned surgical gloves, she folded back the bedcovers and helped Lisa to lift the T-shirt she was wearing and remove her briefs. Then she stood alongside the bed, holding Lisa's hand, while the consultant carried out his examination.

'You know,' he said casually as he pressed Lisa's abdomen, 'this ward gets more like a florist's shop every day.' He nodded towards a huge jug of flowers on the window-sill behind Lisa's bed. 'You can smell the scent from those sweet peas outside in the corridor. And I don't doubt your husband will be bringing even more flowers when he comes to visit you.'

'I hope so.' Lisa managed a smile.

'What are your favourites?' asked Paul Grantham, and while Lisa was thinking about it, he carefully but swiftly completed his examination.

Catherine, watching the gentle compassion of the man and his fine surgeon's hands as they moved over the young woman's body, found it hard to imagine him being furious with his son for being suspended from his school. On the other hand, hadn't she, too, seen just a glimpse of the other side of this man's nature?

'Violets,' said Lisa. 'I love violets but he won't be able to get violets at this time of year so he'll probably bring roses, cream roses just like I had in my wedding bouquet...' Her eyes filled with tears again and she gripped Catherine's hand even more tightly.

'Have you had any pain, Lisa?'

'Yes, in my back,' she replied. 'Low down just like a period pain.' She looked from Paul Grantham to

Catherine and then back again. 'Oh, is everything going to be all right?' she pleaded. 'Jason and I so want this baby.'

'I think there's every chance that your baby will be all right.' Paul Grantham peeled off the surgical gloves and dropped them into a waste bag. 'We're going to send you down for an ultrasound just to make sure. We'll also do some blood tests and give you some medication, but the most important factor for the time being is that you get plenty of rest.'

'Oh, I will,' Lisa replied fervently. 'I will.'

'I'll come back and see you tomorrow, and don't worry, Lisa.' With a smile he moved out of the cubicle, leaving Catherine to help Lisa adjust her nightclothes and blankets and settle her down more comfortably.

By the time Catherine drew back Lisa's curtains the doctors were with Lizzie at Maria Elliott's bedside so she made her way back to the nurses' station, only to find that Helen Brooker's husband, Colin, had just arrived. Already he looked apprehensive, as if he feared the outcome of this unusual request for his attendance at the hospital.

'Perhaps you'd like to come into the relatives' room, Mr Brooker,' said Catherine. 'Mr Grantham is with a patient at the moment but I'm sure he won't keep you waiting for long.'

'What about Helen?' Colin asked. 'Can I see her now?'

'I expect she'll walk up and join you in the relatives' room,' said Catherine. 'It's nice and sunny in there. I'll go and tell her you're here.'

After showing Colin Brooker to the relatives' room, Catherine hurried back to the nurses' station. Against the constant cacophony of ringing buzzers and phones

Paul Grantham and Simon Andrews were studying some notes.

'Mr Grantham,' she said, and as he turned to look at her, once again she felt as if her heart had turned over.

'Yes, Catherine. What is it?'

She swallowed. 'Colin Brooker has just arrived. He's in the relatives' room.'

'His wife is still on the ward, I believe? Perhaps you would like to go and ask her to accompany you to the relatives' room.'

'Shall I tell her her husband is here?'

'No.' He paused. 'Don't alarm her unnecessarily— she'll think there's some crisis with the children.'

Catherine hurried back onto the ward and found Helen sitting in the chair beside her bed, reading the morning paper. She looked up as Catherine approached.

'Oh, hello,' she said. 'What is it this time? Dressings? Tablets? Suppositories?' Her tone dropped ominously.

'No,' said Catherine, 'nothing like that. We're going for a little walk, Helen.' She deliberately kept her voice matter-of-fact and as cheerful as possible, but she knew there was going to be no easy way of getting through the coming interview.

Together they slowly walked out of the ward and the very short distance down the corridor to the relatives' room. Helen asked no more questions, and in the end Catherine had the feeling she'd guessed the nature of what was happening, for when the door of the relatives' room was opened and they stepped into the bright sunlight, Helen didn't seem unduly surprised to find her husband there in the company of the consultant gynaecologist.

CHAPTER EIGHT

'HE WAS absolutely brilliant. Honestly, Lizzie, I can tell you I was dreading it, the whole thing—Paul Grantham telling Helen and Colin Brooker about the result of her operation, what it means, and what is to be done next. I really didn't even want to be in the room while he told them, I'm such a coward over things like that, but he asked me to stay and I had little option.'

'So what happened?' asked Lizzie curiously. It was the end of their shift and the two staff nurses were making their way to the car park.

'He pulled no punches,' Catherine replied. 'He told them exactly what he'd found and the implications, he spoke with compassion but without sentimentality if you know what I mean. But then, somehow, he seemed to turn the whole thing around as he moved on to what further treatment could be offered by way of chemotherapy, radiotherapy and drug therapy. In the end he filled them with so much hope that they left that room on a complete wave of optimism.'

'He's quite a man, isn't he?' said Lizzie.

Catherine nodded. 'I must admit when I first met him I thought he was one of those consultants who loves to play God and who sets out to charm everyone...'

'And was insufferable into the bargain?' Lizzie threw her a sidelong glance.

Catherine nodded. 'Yes, and that. But I have to admit there's a lot more to him than I thought.'

107

'Even down to him letting you use his piano?'

'Even that.' Catherine laughed.

'You were going to tell me about that,' said Lizzie.

'There's not a lot to tell. He asked me about the help I've been giving his daughter and I happened to say that we'd been forced to do that day's practice in a dressing room but that it had been far from satisfactory because we had no music. Anyway, with that, he asked if we'd like to use the piano at his house. I could hardly believe my ears. Honestly, Lizzie, it's a baby grand, complete with the family photographs on the top in their silver frames—in fact, it's as beautiful as the rest of the house.'

'Is the house dead modern—you know, all glass and bleached driftwood?' asked Lizzie.

'No, nothing like that.' Emphatically Catherine shook her head. 'It's all very expensive-looking, but at the same time it's a family home. There's a huge conservatory and even a tennis court, and what looked like a paddock. And the gardens, well, you've never seen anything like the gardens...'

'Sounds quietly luxurious,' said Lizzie admiringly. 'So was his daughter there?'

'Not when I first got there. She came in a little later with her brother.'

'Her brother?'

'Yes, Theo. He's older than Abbie, about seventeen I would say, he must be that, because he drives a car.'

'I must admit we've never known a lot about Paul Grantham's family life,' mused Lizzie. 'He's an intensely private man. There's never even been the slightest whiff of gossip about him as far as I can recall.'

'And that's how it should be for a family man.' Even

as she spoke Catherine was aware of a stab of something somewhere beneath her ribs that could only be
interpreted as envy. Envy for what Paul Grantham's
wife shared with him.

'It's a wonder there hasn't been more speculation,
what with him being so attractive,' Lizzie went on after
a moment. By this time they had reached Catherine's
car where they lingered awhile.

'Maybe he puts paid to any speculation before it
starts,' said Catherine. 'After all, there can't be much
competition with a wife like his.'

'A wife like his?' Lizzie frowned.

'Yes, I saw her as I was leaving the house,'
Catherine replied. 'She was coming up the drive in a
dark blue convertible. A BMW or a Mercedes, I think.
She was blonde, very glamorous...' She trailed off as
she realised Lizzie was shaking her head. 'What's
wrong?' she said uncertainly.

'I don't know who that was,' said Lizzie, 'but it
certainly wasn't his wife.'

'Oh?' Catherine frowned. 'I just assumed it was.'

'Well, I can assure you it wasn't...because Paul
Grantham hasn't got a wife.'

'Hasn't got a wife?' Another stab, not envy this time,
something more compelling, more urgent.

'No.' Lizzie shook her head. 'Paul Grantham is divorced. We may not know much about his private life
but that's one thing we do know. His wife, apparently,
left him when his children were quite young.'

Catherine drove home in a daze—suddenly everything
had changed. Paul Grantham was no longer forbidden
territory. He wasn't married, he was a free man. She
parked her car and let herself into her cottage and a

sudden inexplicable wave of euphoria hit her. As Teazer ran to greet her she scooped him up into her arms and hugged him, laughing as his soft fur tickled her face.

'He's free, Teazer, he's free.' She laughed breathlessly. 'He isn't married after all.' As the cat began to struggle wildly she set him down on the floor where he proceeded to rub himself around her ankles, pleading for his supper.

Her state of euphoria lasted while she fed Teazer, prepared her own meal, watered her house plants and the tubs of flowers in her garden and even until she'd run her bath, undressed and slipped into the scented water.

And for a time, while she soaked, she allowed her imagination to run riot, imagining what it would be like to be important in Paul Grantham's life. To have him ask her out, to embark on a relationship with him…to become the woman in his life…to be loved by him.

It wasn't difficult to fantasise. The memory of the erotic dream she'd had about him hadn't completely faded and simply served to fuel her imagination even further.

How wonderful it would be to go into work each day secure in the knowledge that she was his woman, to know that everyone else knew that, too, to attend Abbie's opening performance with him and the celebration that would follow, to have him take her to the villa in Spain he was rumoured to own…to have him make love to her night after night…to have him ask her to share his life…

She lay there in her dream world until the water began to turn cold and outside in the garden the shadows began to lengthen, and it was only then that reality began to creep in.

So what if he was free? What difference did that make? He would hardly as much as look at her when he had women around him like the glamorous blonde. Goodness knows who she was. OK, so she wasn't his wife, but that didn't mean to say she wasn't heavily involved with him in some way. The way she'd swung her car into the driveway of his house suggested a sense of familiarity as if she had long established the fact that it was her territory.

Maybe she was his live-in partner, Catherine thought as she stood up and with a little shiver stepped from the bath. Or his fiancée, or even just his girlfriend. Whatever she was, the result would be almost the same as if she had been his wife. Miserably she picked up a bath sheet and wrapped herself in its soft, comforting warmth.

But, a little voice persisted at the back of her mind, supposing she was none of those things. Supposing she'd merely been a neighbour, or a friend, just visiting?

But even that didn't guarantee that he wasn't involved with someone else. Surely an attractive man like Paul Grantham, who was also wealthy and at the top of his profession, would have someone special in his life? And if he hadn't, whatever made her think that she, Catherine Slade was in with a chance?

Slowly she padded from the bathroom into her bedroom where she stood in front of her full-length mirror and let the towel drop to the floor. She didn't have a bad figure, she thought as critically she eyed herself up and down. She was fairly tall, with a tiny waist and full but firm breasts. Her hips she considered to be a little on the wide side, but her legs were long and very slim. Shaking her head, she tossed droplets of water from her hair then smoothed it back from her face.

Would he find her attractive? she wondered. He, a man who was constantly looking at women's bodies and who surely would be a discerning judge.

Not that she would ever know, she thought ruefully as, abandoning her daydreams, she pulled on her bathrobe. There was no chance he would look at her in that way, and if she'd ever thought otherwise then she was sadly deluding herself.

She was brushing her hair, Teazer stretched at full length on the bed beside her, when the phone rang. Because Paul Grantham had been so much in her mind, for one crazy moment she imagined the voice she would hear at the other end would be his.

'Catherine?' It was certainly male, but it didn't have that fine modulated tone she'd become used to hearing.

'Yes?'

'It's Simon.'

Disappointment, ridiculous as that was, almost caused her to ask Simon who, but she stopped herself in time and instead managed to say, 'Simon, hello.'

'Catherine, I was just wondering, are you free on Wednesday evening?'

'Oh, Simon, no, I'm sorry, I'm afraid I'm not.' Somehow she couldn't quite bring herself to say she would be at Paul Grantham's house, helping his daughter with her singing.

'OK.' He paused, as if considering his next move. 'What about Friday?' he said at last.

'Er…no. Rehearsal, I'm afraid…'

'I see.' His tone was cool now, implying somehow

that it was her loss. 'Oh, well, never mind. Some other time maybe.'

'Yes, all right, Simon.' She wanted to tell him to ring Lauren and ask her out, to tell him that Lauren was crazy about him, but somehow she didn't quite dare.

She hung up with a decided sense of relief. Maybe now Simon would get the message that she really didn't want to get involved in any sort of heavy relationship—at least, not with him.

The following morning she couldn't wait to get to work. She wanted to see Paul Grantham again because suddenly now she could view him in a whole new light. Before, he had been forbidden fruit because she had thought he was married. But that had now changed and, in spite of all her misgivings of the previous evening, she still felt a tingle of anticipation as she went onto the ward.

At the end of report, however, she found herself listening in dismay as Sister Marlow informed the staff that Mr Grantham wouldn't be in that day, or the next, because he was attending a seminar in Oxford.

Two whole days to get through without seeing him! She could hardly believe it. She had to wait now until she went to his house, and even then there was no guarantee he would be there. He might not be back from the seminar. Disappointment settled on her like a pall and persisted throughout that day and the next.

On the ward, Edna McBride at last was discharged. She was mortified to learn that Mr Grantham wasn't on duty.

'But I wanted to see him,' she said.

I know the feeling, thought Catherine wryly.

'I wanted to thank him personally,' Edna went on.

Helen Brooker continued to recuperate from her operation, but as the optimism inspired by Paul Grantham inevitably waned slightly, she experienced some very low moments when she grew weepy. Catherine sat with her on more than one occasion and allowed her to pour out her grief, anger and understandable fear of the future.

Lisa Wallace continued to rest and suffered no more blood loss. 'It looks like her baby is safe,' said Sister Marlow to her assembled staff, 'but we'll keep her a little longer just to be on the safe side.'

On the doctors' ward round Simon deliberately seemed to avoid Catherine, which saddened her. 'I don't know why we can't just be friends,' she said later to Lizzie.

'Because simple friendship never features on Simon's agenda, that's why,' Lizzie replied with a grin. Growing serious, she said, 'Has he asked you out again?'

'Yes, he has.' Catherine sighed.

'So are you going?'

'Well, the first night he wanted me to go I'd already arranged to help Abbie with her singing, and the second night I have a rehearsal.'

'And you wonder why he's cool with you?' Lizzie gave a short laugh. 'I tell you, Catherine, our Simon simply isn't used to getting the brush off from a woman—any woman. Usually it's the other way round. He does the dumping.'

Somehow she got through those two days and at last, with a steadily mounting sense of anticipation, she found herself making her way to Woodstock.

This time, instead of parking in the lane, she drove between the black gateposts and up the drive, and as she did so she was suddenly swamped by a feeling of familiarity, together with that sense of longing which she'd experienced ever since her return to Langbury.

Rounding the bend in the drive, the first thing she saw on approaching the house was the dark grey Jaguar parked in front of the double garage. Did that indicate that Paul Grantham was home? She tried to dismiss the sudden shaft of excitement that shot through her because, after all, it could merely mean that he had chosen to travel to Oxford by train and hadn't yet returned. Carefully she parked her car alongside the Jaguar, switched off the engine and climbed out.

It was a warm evening with no breeze, and she'd chosen to wear a long cotton skirt in a small floral print together with a close-fitting white top. She felt cool and knew she looked good but her heart was thudding uncomfortably by the time she rang the brass bell alongside the front door. Last time she'd done this there had been no reply. This time, however, the door was opened almost immediately and Abbie stood there, long limbed and golden in shorts and a skimpy top, her blonde hair scrunched untidily onto the top of her head.

'Catherine!' There was pleasure and laughter in those lovely violet eyes. 'Come in. I was just saying to Dad that you would be here soon.'

So he was here. Again that leap of excitement.

'Dad's been to a seminar,' said Abbie as she closed the front door behind Catherine, 'but you would know that. He hasn't been back long. He said it was the most boring seminar he's ever attended.'

'I'm not sure you should be telling that to a member of my staff.' And suddenly he was there, in the hallway, before her. He'd already changed from the suit he must have worn to Oxford and now wore black jeans and a T-shirt. He was smiling and looking incredibly relaxed for a man who'd spent two days being bored.

'I won't say anything if you don't,' said Catherine. She hoped her voice sounded normal but she had the horrible feeling it had come out as a high-pitched squeak. He didn't seem to notice, however, and led the way into the sitting-room. The piano in the bay window was bathed in the evening sunlight.

'There you are,' he said. 'It's all yours.'

'Thank you, Mr Grantham. We'll try not to disturb you too much.'

'That's OK.' He smiled. 'And the name's Paul, by the way.' He turned to his daughter. 'Theo and I will carry on with the barbeque, Abbie. Maybe you can persuade Catherine to join us after your practice if she doesn't have to rush away.'

'Oh, that's a good idea.' Abbie turned to Catherine. 'Can you join us?' she demanded.

'Well, I...' There was nothing she would have liked better, but she didn't want to appear too eager. As it was she was still recovering from him telling her to use his first name. Wait till she told Lizzie that one.

'Oh, go on, please...' Abbie persisted.

'Well, if you're sure I won't be intruding...'

'It's only us and a few friends.'

'All right, then. Thank you.' Catherine smiled, hoping a smile would disguise the awful thumping of her heart which had started again when she'd caught sight of Paul and had grown almost out of control at the thought of spending the evening here with him. Then, in a determined effort to pull herself together, she said, 'So, Abbie, shall we get on?'

'Oh, yes.' Crossing to the piano, Abbie lifted the lid. 'I've already put out the music,' she said.

Catherine set down her bag, took her seat on the piano stool and flexed her fingers, before touching the keys. It played like a dream, the notes clear and pure as Abbie began her vocal warm-up, travelling effortlessly up and down the scales.

Gradually they progressed from scales to exercises, then to the songs from the show, spending the most time on Abbie's solo number. The sitting-room windows were open and as her voice soared the sweet, clear sound must have traveled far on the still air of the summer's evening.

And as the lesson progressed the scent of roses from beneath the bay window was gradually replaced by another smell, the mouth-watering smoky smell of food being cooked on an open barbeque.

'That's making me feel very hungry,' said Abbie at last.

'Me, too,' Catherine admitted. 'I think it's time we called it a day.'

'How am I doing?' asked Abbie as Catherine began collecting up the sheet music.

'So much better. I can hardly believe how much you've improved.'

'It's all thanks to you,' said Abbie. 'I really am grateful, Catherine. And it's so kind of you to give up your time to come here.' While Catherine sought a suitable reply, Abbie went on, 'Shall we go into the garden and join the others?'

Closing the lid of the piano, Catherine followed Abbie from the sitting-room into the conservatory and out of the French doors.

Theo was standing before the barbeque, grilling

steaks and sausages, while his father was pouring drinks for a small group of people, none of whom Catherine had seen before. One or two of the younger ones she imagined to be friends of Abbie and Theo, and as Abbie made a beeline for a tall girl with red hair who was talking to a couple of boys on the lawn Catherine stood uncertainly for a moment on the terrace.

It was Paul who caught sight of her and beckoned her forward. 'Catherine,' he said as she reached his side, and for one crazy, almost unbelievable moment he took her arm, his fingers cool against her bare flesh. 'Come and meet some people. They are mostly neighbours,' he added by way of explanation.

He introduced her to first one then another of the people present. 'This is Catherine,' he said. 'She's a friend of Abbie's and has very kindly agreed to help Abbie with her singing.' He didn't mention the fact that Catherine, was also a member of his staff.

'Well, you must be doing a very good job,' said one elderly lady, 'if what we heard just now is an example.'

'Yes, Abbie, darling,' said another, 'you sing like an angel. We can't wait to see your show. *Oliver!*, isn't it? We're all coming.'

'Keep talking,' said Abbie with a laugh. 'You might even persuade my father to come.'

'Paul?' The elderly lady turned in surprise to look at him. 'What's all this? Surely you'll be going to Abbie's show? Aren't you proud of her?'

'He doesn't like show business,' said Abbie, pulling a face. 'Do you, Pops?'

'Well, here's someone who might persuade him even if the rest of us can't,' someone else chipped in before Paul himself had a chance to answer. As they all turned to see who it was who had just entered the garden by the side gate, Catherine suddenly froze. She hardly had to turn to see because, somehow, she knew who it would be.

'Faye.' He went to meet her, kissing her Continental-style on both cheeks, and Catherine's heart sank. She might not be his wife but quite obviously she was someone who was very important in his life. Tonight she wore black crêpe trousers and a matching sleeve-less top, and her hair was loose.

All those present seemed to know the woman, which led Catherine to wonder if she, too, was a neighbour. Then as greetings were exchanged Paul turned. 'Catherine,' he said, 'this is Faye Elton. Faye, I'd like you to meet Catherine Slade. Catherine is helping Abbie with her singing.'

Catherine was aware of a cool little nod, a veiled expression in a pair of green eyes, and then the woman had moved on, past Catherine, to take the drink that Paul had poured for her, her fingers lingeringly touch-ing his.

The setting was glorious, music drifted from the house and as the shadows began to lengthen, Abbie drew Catherine over to the barbeque where Theo placed a juicy piece of steak, some spiced chicken and herb filled sausage onto their plates. 'Help yourselves to salads,' he said.

His blue eyes and dark hair made a startling and unusual combination, and as Catherine made her way to a wooden seat beneath the pergola she was struck once again by the fact that this was how Paul must have looked at the same age.

The food was delicious, and as Catherine finished

hers and was licking her fingers she was joined by Theo. 'Hi,' he said. 'Can I get you anything else?'

'No. No, thank you.' Catherine shook her head. 'That was wonderful, Theo, delicious. You're an excellent barbeque chef.'

'And you must be an excellent singing teacher—I couldn't believe that was Abbie singing just now. I had no idea she could produce sounds like that.'

'She has a wonderful voice,' replied Catherine, 'but, believe me, it's nothing to do with me. Tell me…' She threw him a sidelong glance. 'Do you sing?'

'Lord, no!' Theo shook his head and the dark hair fell across his forehead. 'I think I'm tone deaf—I probably take after Dad.'

'And Abbie?'

'Oh, Abbie takes after our mother—no doubt about that.'

'Really?' Catherine spoke casually but she was aware of a quickening of interest.

'Yes, she was involved in the theatre,' Theo went on.

'Do you mean professionally?' asked Catherine in surprise. Could this be the reason for Paul's antipathy?

Theo frowned, his profile achingly like his father's. 'No, just amateur dramatics…I think. I don't really know a lot about it. I was only ten when my parents separated but I do remember my mother singing a lot and playing the piano.'

'Is she still involved?' asked Catherine curiously.

'I don't know.' Theo shook his head. 'She married again after she and my father divorced and she lives in America now.'

'Do you see her?' The question was out before she

had time to even consider whether or not it was one she should have asked.

Theo shook his head. 'No,' he said. As his gaze met hers she thought she detected a sadness in his eyes. 'No, we don't see her. She wanted us to visit her about a year ago but Dad wasn't keen for us to go.'

'But what about you? What did you want?'

He shrugged. 'Don't know really. It's been a long time and I guess there are some things that are best left alone.'

At that moment Catherine looked up and saw Paul approaching them across the terrace. She rose to her feet. It really wouldn't do to appear to be outstaying her welcome.

'I must be going,' she said, glancing at her watch, the implication being that she had a pressing engagement elsewhere when, in actual fact, if she was honest, there was no where else on earth she would rather be.

'So soon?' said Paul softly as Theo also rose to his feet, murmuring an excuse and slipping away to join the young people who were heading in the direction of the tennis court.

'Yes, really…'

'I'll walk to your car with you,' he replied.

Several people called goodbye as together they crossed the terrace and Catherine was aware of smiles and nods from most. But as they passed Faye Elton on their way to the wrought-iron gate set in the wall, there was no smile or nod, simply that bland expression on her features that had been there before.

CHAPTER NINE

'THANK you for the barbeque,' Catherine said when they reached her car. It was quiet here at the front of the house, away from the music and the sound of voices and laughter in the garden. Catherine was aware of the dark blue BMW parked on the far side of the Jaguar, and as she unlocked the door of her own little car she was suddenly hard pushed to know what else to say.

'Not at all,' Paul replied. 'It was nice that you could join us. But we can't impose on any more of your time. No doubt your company is greatly in demand.'

'Not really…'

'No hot date tonight?' He raised his eyebrows and she met that tantalising blue gaze.

'No.' She shook her head.

'But you said you had to go. I imagined you would be meeting someone special.'

'No.' She shook her head again, suddenly acutely aware of his closeness as he held the car door open for her. 'There's no one special.'

'I find that hard to believe.' He spoke softly but there was something different, some new element that had entered his tone.

Startled, she glanced up and found his gaze roaming over her, taking in her clothes, her hair, her face and finally coming to rest on her mouth. 'I would have thought,' he added, 'you might have been meeting my SHO tonight.'

'I don't know whatever gave you that idea.' Desperately she tried to keep her tone casual, but found it difficult because that would have been so at odds with the pounding of her heart.

'Well, correct me if I'm wrong, but I was under the distinct impression that you and Simon were an item.'

'Who told you that?' She allowed her gaze to meet his, which had moved now from her mouth.

'I'm not sure that anyone actually told me. Call it observation.' He shrugged. 'Or hospital gossip.'

'You can't always believe hospital gossip.'

'Maybe not. But…' he paused '…I thought you and Simon went out together recently.'

'Yes,' she agreed lightly, wondering how on earth he knew that, 'we did. But it was only the once.'

'Not to be repeated?' He looked surprised now. 'Simon gave the impression it was very much an on-going situation.'

'Maybe *he* thought it was.'

'But you didn't?'

'Let's just say I didn't want him getting the wrong impression.'

'So are you saying you've turned him down?'

'I may have done.'

'Well, I would think that has to be a first.' He appeared amused now.

'That's what Lizzie Rowe said.'

'So that leaves you—where? At a loose end? You seemed in a hurry.'

'I have things to do.'

'Ah, yes, of course. And I have detained you long enough,' he said. 'I must let you go.' But he didn't move, continuing to stand close to her, holding her car door open.

In the end it was Catherine who from somewhere found the motivation to slip into the driver's seat, and eventually Paul was forced to move to close the door. She wound down the window and looked up at him. 'Are you on duty tomorrow?' she asked.

He nodded. 'Yes. I'll see you on the unit.'

'All right.' She smiled and turned the key in the ignition.

'Goodbye, Catherine.'

'Goodbye...Paul.'

Carefully she reversed her car. It wouldn't do to hit the Jaguar or, heaven forbid, the BMW. Then she was away. He raised his hand in farewell. She glanced twice in her driving mirror. The first time he was standing there in the drive, simply watching her drive away, but the second time he had been joined by Faye Elton who, no doubt, had come to see what was keeping him and who now, with her arm tucked into his, was drawing him back into the garden.

In spite of that, Catherine felt as if she was on some sort of a high as she drove home because now, and perhaps for the first time, Paul seemed to have shown a personal interest in her. He had asked her to use his first name, he had invited her to stay for the barbeque and then, during those last few moments they had spent alone, he had questioned her about her private life and about whether or not there was anyone special. And he had seemed so interested, pleased even when she had told him there wasn't, that there was nothing between herself and Simon.

But wasn't this just Paul Grantham's style? Didn't everyone think they were special to him, hadn't all his patients said that he treated them like they were the only one?

She mustn't read too much into this, she tried to tell herself as she drove back to Langbury. But there was no denying the excitement she felt for now not only had she established the fact that he wasn't married but he also seemed to be taking an interest in her personally over and above his paternal interest in what she was doing for Abbie and quite aside from their professional involvement.

There was still Faye Elton to consider and Catherine remained uncertain what role she played in Paul Grantham's life, but she refused to allow the thought of that to mar either the happiness she was feeling as a result of that evening or the anticipation that was slowly building at the thought of seeing him the following day at work.

For the next few days Catherine seemed to float along on the same cloud. At work she lived for those moments when Paul came onto the ward, and when she was at home she counted the days until the time she would once again visit his home.

To any casual onlooker there was no obvious change in her relationship with the consultant, but Lizzie was no casual onlooker, and it was while they were waiting to admit two new patients to the ward one morning that she tackled Catherine. The doctors had just finished their ward round and had disappeared to the theatre to scrub up, but before they had gone, Paul Grantham had paused for a quiet word with Catherine.

'What was all that about?' asked Lizzie afterwards.

'All what about?' Catherine feigned innocence.

'Mr Grantham getting you in the corner for a cosy little chat.'

'He didn't!' Catherine protested.

'Well, it certainly looked that way from where I was standing. So what did he want?'

'It was only a message from his daughter about me going to the house for a lesson...'

'Oh, yes, I'd forgotten about that,' said Lizzie. 'So it's all fixed, then, for you to go there?'

'Er, yes.' Catherine paused. 'Actually, I've done one already...'

'Well, you're a dark horse.' Lizzie turned and stared at her. 'You didn't say! How did it go?'

'All right.' Catherine nodded.

'So, is that it? Just all right. Aren't you going to tell me any more?'

'What else do you want to know?'

'Well, who was there? Was *he* there—Mr Grantham?'

'Yes.' Catherine nodded. 'And his son, Theo.'

'What's he like?' asked Lizzie curiously. 'Is he like his dad?'

'Yes, sort of.' Catherine wrinkled her nose. 'He's certainly good-looking, and very dark, and I would say he's a bit of a charmer so, no doubt, he gets that from his father. He also told me he's tone deaf and that apparently is inherited from his father.'

'That must have been some chat you had. Was he sitting in on the lesson?' asked Lizzie.

'Oh, no, this was after the lesson,' said Catherine. 'Theo was cooking the food for the barbeque—'

'Barbeque?' Lizzie's eyes became round. 'What barbeque?'

'They were having a barbeque—the Granthams,' Catherine explained. Already she was wishing she hadn't mentioned the word 'barbeque' because she knew Lizzie wouldn't leave it there.

'And were you included in this barbeque?'

'Well, yes, as a matter of fact, I was.'

'So who asked you to that? Abbie?'

'Well, Abbie wanted me to stay, but it was actually Paul's idea…'

'Oh, so it's Paul now, is it?' Lizzie's eyes widened even more.

'Shh.' Catherine glanced over her shoulder. 'Yes, he told me to call him Paul, but I would say that's only when I go to the house with Abbie. I suppose he thought it sounded too formal for me to keep calling him Mr Grantham while everyone else was calling him Paul.' She paused. 'I wouldn't call him Paul here, though. He's still Mr Grantham at work.'

'I'm glad to hear it.' A gleam of amusement had entered Lizzie's eyes. 'So who else was at this barbeque?'

'There were several others there. Mostly neighbours, I think, and some young people who were friends of Abbie and Theo.'

'And was *she* there?'

'She?'

'Yes, the glamorous blonde in the convertible.'

'Oh, her. Yes, she was, as a matter of fact.'

'So who is she? Did you find out?'

'Not really.' Catherine shrugged. 'Her name is Faye Elton. Everyone seemed to know her so I dare say she, too, was a neighbour.'

'How long did you stay?'

'Not too long. I ate my food then went soon after. Didn't want to outstay my welcome.'

'And now you're all set for the next time.'

'Yes. I suppose I am.'

'Catherine?'

'Mmm?'

'Be careful, won't you?'

'What do you mean? What is there to be careful about?'

'I'm afraid you might get hurt,' said Lizzie gently.

'Hurt? Why should I get hurt? Of course I won't get hurt. I don't know what you mean.'

'Oh, I think you do,' Lizzie replied.

One of that day's new admissions to the ward was Valerie Ogilvie, a lady of forty-five who had been experiencing much pain and discomfort and who was to undergo a laparoscopy to investigate the causes.

'I thought at first it was just symptoms of the menopause,' she told Catherine, 'but now it seems more than that. My GP suggested it might be endometriosis.'

'Well, a laparoscopy will show the surgeon what might be wrong.'

'I was having really heavy periods, then they stopped for a few months and now they're back again as heavy as ever. When they first stopped I simply thought it was the change, and then I panicked and thought I might be pregnant.'

'Would that have been such a disaster?' asked Catherine with a smile.

'At my age! You must be joking. I have two grandchildren, for heaven's sake,' Valerie replied, rolling her eyes in horror.

'A lot of women are having babies later in life.'

'Not this one.' Valerie gave a short laugh. 'I dare say it might be all right for some of these celebrities or high-flying career women who delay having their families, but even then I think they might get a shock when faced with the reality of a demanding baby. And just imagine coping with stroppy teenagers when you're drawing your pension! No, I really don't think life was meant to be like that. I enjoyed having my children and bringing them up when I was young and full of energy. I couldn't do it now, neither would I want to.' She paused and looked questioningly at Catherine. 'Do you have children, Nurse?'

'No. I'm not married...'

'Well, that doesn't seem to make much difference these days either, but do you want children?'

'Oh, yes. Yes, I would like a family one day.'

'Take my advice and don't leave it too long. Have them while you are young enough to enjoy them.'

Catherine found herself wondering whether that applied to fathers as well. Paul Grantham had had his family. He must be in his forties. How would he feel about starting again?

But what difference could it possibly make to her how he felt? She tried to put him out of her mind and concentrate on her work, but time and again her thoughts would return to him, and even if she did manage to think about other things for a while something would happen, like Paul putting in an unexpected appearance on the ward to visit a patient, and she would be right back at square one again.

And those moments when she observed him with a patient were very special because they showed that caring, compassionate side of his nature which she so admired. She would watch him as he stood at the foot of a patient's bed, talking to them, dressed in a dark suit and a white shirt. He wouldn't always be wearing a tie and more often than not the top two buttons of his shirt would be undone.

Sometimes she would catch a glimpse of him in

Theatre as he stood in his greens, complete with mask, as he waited to receive a patient, and then again he would come back to the ward after a long day operating to check on a patient's progress. On those occasions he would be wearing an unbuttoned white coat worn loosely over shirt and trousers, and he would slip quietly into a curtained-off cubicle and stay beside the bed for a while, the patient's hand in his as he stood looking down at them.

Catherine wasn't sure at what point she realised she was falling in love with Paul. It might have been when Lizzie had told her to be careful, it might have been during one of the visits to his home, or it might have been right back at the beginning and the first time she had looked into those incredibly blue eyes. She really didn't know.

The only thing she did know was that it was happening and there was nothing she could do about it. It was the main reason why she had felt unable to allow any relationship to develop between Simon and herself. And while being only too aware of the pitfalls of the situation, she also recognised that what was happening was somehow tied up with those strange but intense feelings of anticipation and of waiting for someone that she'd experienced since returning to Langbury.

At times the improbability of it all would wash over her and it was at those times that the future looked bleak, but for the most part she was willing to let her feelings ride and to get used to the idea that she had fallen in love with Paul, even if that love might never be returned.

Then, as time went on, she even began to wonder if there was a chance, however slight, that he might come to care for her. He was older than her, but did that matter? A lot of women had relationships with older men—even married them. He was her boss, but did that matter either, provided it didn't interfere with their work? There was also the indomitable Faye Elton in the background, but no one had actually come right out and said she was in a relationship with Paul, so until it became a proven fact that was where she would let her remain—firmly in the background.

This wave of optimism would last for a time, only to be replaced by a surge of despair when she remembered that even if all obstacles were removed there was absolutely no guarantee that Paul felt the same way about her as she did about him. His attitude had certainly changed towards her from the time he had challenged her for filling his daughter's head with nonsense to getting to know her outside their working environment and appearing to actually appreciate the interest she was showing in Abbie. At times she felt that interest showed a hint of something deeper, like the time he had lingered with her at her car, asking about her personal life, and sometimes on the ward when he seemed to single her out either by a look or a smile which she fervently hoped was for her alone.

There was no knowing how long things might have gone on like this, and the day that brought about a change began like any other with no hint of what was to come.

It was a day that she was to go to the Granthams to give Abbie a lesson in the evening, so for that reason alone it started on a note of optimism. The only difference to any other day was the fact that on her way to work Catherine took her car into a local garage for an MOT and a service.

'I'll ring you after my shift to see what time I can

pick it up,' she told the mechanic. She set off to walk from the garage to the hospital and had only gone a short distance when a car passed her, then stopped a few yards further on up the road. It was almost as if the driver hadn't intended stopping then had thought better of it. Catherine didn't recognise the car, and as she drew alongside and bent down in order to look at the driver she was surprised to see that it was no other than Lauren.

'Hello, Lauren,' she said opening the door.

'Are you going to work?' her colleague asked.

'Yes, I've just dropped my car off at the garage.'

'Hop in, I'll give you a lift.'

'Thanks.' Catherine slipped into the passenger seat and closed the door. 'It's a bit of a trek up that hill.'

They were mostly silent and Catherine, remembering Lauren's coolness towards her and the reason for it, found herself wondering if there was some way that she could let her know she simply wasn't interested in Simon. Her opportunity came as they approached the hospital and passed a poster advertising the annual Summer Ball. 'Are you going to that?' she asked the younger girl.

'Don't know.' Lauren shrugged. 'Depends if I'm asked. I suppose you are.' Her tone was a mixture of envy and wistfulness, and Catherine found herself wishing she could say that she was going and that it was Paul Grantham who had asked her.

Instead, she said, 'Oh, I don't know. I doubt it. No one's asked me and I don't like going to these things alone.'

Lauren was silent for a moment then with a little frown she said, 'I thought you would be going with Simon.'

'Simon?' Deliberately Catherine frowned. 'Oh, you mean Simon Andrews? Lord, no. Whatever gave you that idea?'

'Well, I thought…I thought you and he…'

'Were an item?' Did the whole hospital believe this to be true? Catherine thought in a sudden surge of exasperation. 'No, not at all. Nothing like that.'

'Oh,' said Lauren. 'Oh, I see.'

'Maybe you should ask Simon to go with you,' said Catherine lightly. 'After all, these days it doesn't seem to matter who asks who.'

'I don't know about that…' Lauren looked doubtful.

'Go on—live dangerously.' Catherine laughed.

'Well, maybe I will at that.' Lauren grew decidedly more cheerful after that and by the time they'd parked in the staff car park, to Catherine's amusement, she was positively chatty.

It was a busy morning on the ward, with new admissions, a theatre list and two discharges.

One patient on the theatre list was to have a myomectomy, or removal of fibroids, another was for a hysterectomy and the third for a termination of pregnancy. This last patient, Mel Deacon, was in a highly distressed state as she and her husband had been eager to start a family, but in the twelfth week of her pregnancy she had contracted rubella and it was possible the baby had been affected. After much soul-searching and counselling it had been agreed that termination was necessary. Lizzie was preparing her for Theatre while Catherine prepared Annette Weeks for her fibroid operation.

'I'll be so glad to get all this sorted out at last,' she told Catherine. 'My periods have been horrendous. I haven't been able to do anything. Goodness knows how much longer they will keep my job open. I'm just counting on Mr Grantham to put everything right for me.'

'Which, of course, he will,' said Catherine. 'Now, I want you to have your bath, then put on this theatre gown. Afterwards I'll give you your pre-med to help you to relax.'

She hadn't seen Paul yet that morning but just the mention of his name caused her heart to miss a beat and the anticipation continued to grow until the moment when she accompanied Annette Weeks to Theatre and he was there in the anaesthetics room. It was almost as if he had known it was to be her on escort duty that morning, as if he were waiting there just to see her.

Which, of course, was ridiculous. Why would he do that? Far more likely that he had just wandered out of the scrub room to speak to Sanjay Patel who was preparing his medication trolley.

But, whatever the reason, he was there, and as Catherine passed her patient over to the theatre staff nurse he looked up, his gaze meeting hers, and she felt herself melt. He wasn't yet wearing his mask, which hung loosely around his neck, but his hair was covered by his theatre cap and he wore his theatre greens and clogs.

'Hello, Catherine,' he said softly as she would have turned to leave the anaesthetics room.

'Hello.' Her voice was little more than a whisper. She would have liked to have called him by his name, but she didn't quite dare, not here where other members of staff were present.

'I understand we are to see you this evening.'

'Yes.' She nodded.

'I trust you'll stay for supper?'

'I'd love to. Thank you.'

That was all. But it was more than enough to put her on a high for the rest of the day.

Somehow she got through the shift. In due course she collected Annette Weeks from the recovery room and escorted her back to the ward, where she and Tiffany washed and dressed her in her own nightdress and carried out half-hourly observations. She sat with Mel Deacon when she came round from the anaesthetic following her termination, holding her hand and comforting her. This particular case had really touched Catherine and her heart went out to Mel as she wept for the loss of her baby.

She admitted two new patients, one who was to have a salpingectomy and oophorectomy, or removal of the ovaries and Fallopian tubes, and another who was suffering from pelvic inflammatory disease and adhesions caused by previous surgery.

It was while completing the paperwork on these patients that Lizzie caught up with her in the nurses' station. 'You look like the cat that got the cream,' she said with a grin.

'Do I?' said Catherine innocently. 'I can't think why.'

'Wouldn't be a Woodstock evening by any chance, I suppose?'

'As a matter of fact, yes, it is, but—'

'Well, there you are, then. And talking of cats getting the cream—Lauren's as bad. I can't get any sense out of her this morning.'

'Ah, now, I may know the reason for that,' Catherine replied. 'I told Lauren this morning that there isn't anything between me and Simon—she was under the impression we were practically living together. I think they may get it together again now.'

'Let's hope she doesn't live to regret it,' said Lizzie drily.

'What do you mean?' Catherine frowned.

'He'll use her,' Lizzie replied. 'And break her heart just like he has all the others.'

At last the shift came to an end and Catherine rang the garage to see at what time she could pick up her car, only to be told that there was further work to be done on it, that they had to purchase a part and that the work wouldn't be completed until the following day.

It wasn't until after she'd hung up that with a pang of dismay she realised that without a car she wouldn't be able to get to Woodstock that evening.

CHAPTER TEN

CATHERINE'S heart had started to thud while she was putting her key in the lock, and by the time she had let herself into her cottage, picked up the phone, dialled the number and heard the phone ringing at the other end, her pulse was racing. Teazer must have wondered what was wrong with her for her greeting had fallen far short of what he was used to on her return from work.

Probably Abbie would answer, she thought, or maybe Theo, which meant she was getting herself into a state for nothing.

'Hello?'

'Oh, hello.' Her mouth went dry. 'Is that…is that Paul?'

'Yes.'

'Paul, it's Catherine.'

'Hello, Catherine.' Had his tone softened slightly, or was it her imagination?

'Paul, I'm sorry, but I'm not going to be able to come over this evening.'

There was silence at the other end of the line. 'Is there a problem?' he asked.

'I don't have any transport. My car went into the garage this morning and unfortunately it won't be ready until tomorrow.'

'That isn't a problem. I'll come and pick you up.'

She swallowed, with difficulty because her mouth

and throat were still very dry. 'Oh, I couldn't expect you to do that...'

'Nonsense. Of course I will. After all, it's you who's doing the favour for Abbie. I'll be over at six-thirty.'

It was obvious by his tone that the matter was closed. 'All right,' she replied weakly.

She found herself getting ready with great care, just as if she were getting ready for a heavy date. Which was crazy because this wasn't a date by any means. Paul might be picking her up, and he might have asked her to stay for supper—he might also, presumably, be bringing her home—but that still didn't mean it was a date.

Nevertheless, by the time she had decided on a long, saffron-coloured dress, which she knew looked good with her dark hair, her bedroom looked as if it had been under siege, with the contents of her wardrobe strewn across her bed as she had discarded first one then another garment in her frantic attempt to find the right clothes to wear.

She was ready a good half-hour before he was due, then spent the rest of the time darting backwards and forwards to the front window of the cottage to see if he had arrived. When there was barely two minutes to go to the appointed time, she dashed back upstairs in an agony of indecision and changed first her shoes and then her earrings. By the time she came back downstairs the dark grey Jaguar was at the gate.

Taking a deep breath, she opened the front door, raised her hand in acknowledgement, shut the door behind her then strolled down the path in what she hoped was a relaxed and unhurried way.

He had got out of the car and was holding the door open for her, watching her as she approached. She was unused to such chivalry and after he had greeted her, waiting while she slid into the passenger seat then shutting the door behind her, she looked up, glimpsed the admiration in his eyes and suddenly felt special, fragile even, and very, very feminine.

Moments later he was sitting beside her, and as she sank back into the car's soft leather upholstery he started the engine and they drew away from the cottage.

'This is very good of you,' she said tentatively, unsure how the conversation would proceed.

'Not at all. It's the least I can do. Besides, Abbie would have been very disappointed if you hadn't been able to come.'

'She's doing very well, you know,' she said wildly, desperate now for some safe topic.

'I know very little of these matters,' he said, 'but I have to say, from what I've heard when she's been practising, I would be inclined to agree with you.'

'You will come to the opening night of the show, won't you?' She threw him an anxious, sidelong glance. He was casually dressed tonight in pale grey trousers and a cream cashmere sweater, and to Catherine he looked achingly handsome. His strong, capable hands lightly held the steering-wheel and so stirred were her emotions as she stared at them that she was forced to transfer her gaze to his face once more.

'I rather think I won't have any option.' His eyes crinkled at the corners.

'You'll enjoy it,' said Catherine. 'It's a wonderful show and Abbie is an absolute delight.'

'Abbie tells me you're auditioning for the lead in the company's next performance.' It was his turn to glance at her.

She nodded. 'Maybe you'll come to that one as well.'

'Maybe I will at that.' He smiled again and Catherine found herself trying to imagine just how she would feel should she be successful at audition, performing the part of Eliza Doolittle in front of Paul. The idea was so overwhelming that she was forced to abandon it before it intimidated her completely.

'Is your talent inherited?' he asked curiously as they left Langbury behind and took the Woodstock road.

'My father was in show business,' she replied briefly.

'Did he encourage you?'

'When I was very small he did, but after my parents separated I didn't see a lot of my father.'

'Did that bother you?'

'Yes, it did, actually. I missed him very much.'

He was silent after that for a long while then as they were approaching the outskirts of Woodstock he spoke again. 'You realise, of course, that I'm divorced?'

'Yes, I know.'

'My children no longer see their mother.'

'I think that's very sad,' she replied quietly.

'Things aren't that simple,' he said.

'No, I'm sure they aren't. These things never are.'

He said no more then and the matter was dropped as he drew into the drive and parked the Jaguar in front of the garage. Catherine climbed from the car and Abbie came out of the house to greet them.

The practice went well and when it was over, to Catherine's surprise, Abbie informed her that she and Theo had been invited to a friend's house for the evening. 'But you're having supper with Dad,' she ended, and just for one moment Catherine thought she de-

tected a note of triumph in the girl's voice, almost as
if she and her brother had somehow engineered the
whole thing.

Abbie and Theo left almost immediately and
Catherine found herself alone in the kitchen with Paul.

'I hadn't realised they were going out,' she said, as
through the kitchen window they watched Abbie and
Theo drive away in his car. 'I can go if you like.'

'What, and waste all this pasta I've prepared?' Paul
looked indignant, but Catherine got the impression that
he had known his children were going out. Whether or
not he had known it when he'd invited her to stay was
another matter.

'I thought we'd eat in the conservatory,' he said as
he took a bottle of wine from a rack on the wall.

'Wonderful,' said Catherine weakly. She was still
trying to come to terms with the unbelievable fact that
she was to be alone with him for at least part of the
evening.

'Take a seat.' He indicated a stool. 'It won't be long
now. Let me pour you a drink.'

Helplessly she watched him as, with an almost feline
grace, he moved around the large kitchen, pouring
drinks—red Chianti—into tall goblets, preparing salad,
checking on the pasta and cooking a delicious, aro-
matic sauce. She could still hardly believe this was
happening, that she was actually here alone with him
in his home. She was afraid that at any moment she
would wake up or, even worse, that Faye Elton might
suddenly appear and announce that she, too, had come
for supper.

But when eventually they went through to the conservatory she saw to her relief that the white wrought-
iron table in the far corner was set for two. There were

blue candles on the table, floating in a cut-glass bowl, and Catherine wondered if Abbie had been responsible for those, along with an arrangement of daisies and cornflowers. The tableware was exquisite, a snowy white cloth and napkins, silver cutlery and sparkling cut glass. Soft music played in the background and the French doors stood open to admit the heady scent of the jasmine and white roses that tumbled over the pergola.

Paul escorted her to her seat and with a laugh and a flourish arranged her napkin on her lap.

The food was delicious, perfectly cooked, and complemented by Paul's choice of wine. The conversation was easy, touching briefly on hospital matters but moving swiftly on to holidays.

'The hospital grapevine says you have a villa in Spain,' said Catherine after she had told him of the few Continental holidays she had enjoyed.

'That's right.' He nodded. 'It's my luxury, my retreat from the hectic schedule that my life has become. It's the most perfect place, in the hills between Javea and Denia. When I'm there I eat all my meals on the terrace and practically live in the pool. I've made friends with many of the local Spanish people and I visit them in their homes and they in turn visit me.'

'It sounds like paradise,' said Catherine with a sigh.

'Oh, it is,' he replied. 'My own little corner of paradise.'

'Do the children go with you?'

'Yes, usually.' He nodded then took another mouthful of wine. 'But lately I've suspected they'll soon want to do their own thing. I fear family holidays will become a thing of the past. Theo, especially, is starting to show his need for independence, and even my little

Abbie has shown a hint of rebellion, as you well know.' He smiled and inclined his head, then after a moment he added, 'There have been problems with Theo lately.'

'Really?' She feigned surprise, careful not to break Abbie's confidence.

'He was suspended from his school for a week at the end of the term.' Paul spoke almost with relief, as if he had wanted to talk about it but didn't know how or to whom. 'Wild behaviour was the official reason,' he went on, 'which the headmaster informed me was totally unacceptable.'

'Do you know what this wild behaviour amounted to?'

'As far as I can make out, a joyriding jaunt with three other boys in one of the teachers' cars—taken without his consent, I have to add, and driven by Theo who was the only one to hold a driving licence. When they were stopped by the police two of the boys were found to be in possession of cannabis.'

'Oh, Paul, I am sorry.' She stared at him. 'It's no good me saying it was nothing, that all lads do it or that it doesn't matter, because I know how upset you must have been.'

He nodded. 'I was—still am actually, especially as the whole situation is still under review. I suppose there's a very real possibility the school may not take him back next term—and with his A-levels coming up...' He shrugged helplessly.

There was a deep silence in the conservatory and suddenly Catherine felt sorry for this man who, so compassionate over the sufferings of his patients, was now suffering himself over the thoughtless actions of his son.

'Have you and Theo been able to talk?' she asked tentatively at last.

'Some,' he admitted. 'But it hasn't been easy. In fact, if I'm honest, our relationship hasn't been too easy for some time now.'

'Any particular reason for that?'

Paul hesitated before answering, lifting his wineglass and thoughtfully staring at it as he swirled its contents while considering. 'I think it may be to do with his mother,' he said at last.

Catherine found she had been holding her breath as she waited for his answer, and gently she let it out. 'His mother?' she asked quietly.

'Yes.' He paused, as if still uncertain quite how much he should say. 'She contacted us nearly a year ago,' he continued at last. 'She wanted to see the children—wanted them to visit her in the States.'

'And…?'

'Well, it was out of the question—naturally.'

'Why naturally? I would have thought it the most natural thing in the world for a mother to want to see her children.'

There was another long silence between them where the only sounds were the faint click made by some flying insect as it hit one of the conservatory's panes of glass and the soft music from the hidden CD player.

'You don't understand,' said Paul at last.

'I may do,' Catherine replied. 'Why not try me?'

He remained silent again then he appeared to take a deep breath. 'She left them,' he said tightly at last. 'She left them when they were still quite small. She made her choice. There was no contact from her for a very long time apart from birthdays and Christmas. She can't expect to swan back into their lives now as if nothing has happened and expect to pick up where she left off.'

Catherine, watching him as he spoke, for a moment glimpsed the raw emotions of agony and betrayal on his features.

'We've been to hell and back—the three of us,' he admitted at last. 'We've come out of it in the last few years and have been able to get on with our lives. I don't want her ruining it again.'

Catherine was quiet for a moment, reflecting, wondering just how much she dared say to this proud, private man. 'How do Abbie and Theo feel about this?' she asked tentatively at last.

'What do you mean?' He frowned.

'Well, did they want to see their mother when she contacted you?'

He shook his head. 'No,' he said. 'Why should they after what she'd done to them? They were quite indignant at the time, if I recall…'

'And since then?' asked Catherine quietly.

'Well, I don't think they've had reason to change their minds…'

'So you don't think Abbie's rebellion over the theatre, her auditioning without consulting you or Theo's problems at his school might have had anything to do with it?'

He stared at her. 'No, of course not. Absolutely not. Why should they?'

'No reason.' She shrugged. 'I just wondered, that's all.'

'No. I can't see…' He shook his head.

After a while Catherine said, 'Theo told me that Abbie has inherited her theatrical talent from her mother.'

Paul was silent, staring once again at the contents of his wineglass before swallowing them in one mouthful. 'Yes,' he agreed at last, 'I dare say she has.'

'Was her mother a professional?'

He shook his head. 'No, purely amateur…'

'Was she good?'

'Yes, she was,' he admitted. 'She had talent. I used to go and see the productions she was in at one time…until the pressure of work became too great. After that there simply wasn't time.' He fell silent again and intuitively Catherine knew there was no point in pressing him. If he wanted to tell her more he would do so, but in his own time.

'It was how she met him,' he went on at last, 'the man she's now married to. He was in the same productions as her. After she left me they went to America to live. The children stayed with me and she didn't fight for custody. She has two more children now.'

'And you?' she asked softly.

'Me?' he frowned. 'What about me?'

'Do you still love her?'

He drew in his breath sharply and Catherine feared she had gone too far.

'No,' he said at last. 'Not any more. I let go of the love a very long time ago.'

'That's good.' She nodded. 'I wonder, though…' She trailed off as she thought better of what she had been about to say.

'You wonder what?'

'Oh, nothing—it's all right.'

'No, go on,' he persisted. 'What were you going to say? You wonder what?'

'I just wondered, that's all. You say you've let go

of the love, but have you let go of the hurt, the bitter-ness?'

'What do you mean?' His eyes narrowed.

'Simply that.' Catherine shrugged. 'If you're unable to let Theo and Abbie go and see their mother because of what she did to them then, in your heart you're still punishing her. Maybe it's time to let go.'

Paul leaned back in his chair and stared at her across the table. Outside twilight was falling and a couple of bats swooped and dived amongst the trees.

'And you think,' he said at last, 'that my letting go, as you put it, will help Abbie and Theo?'

'Yes, I think it would. They are reaching the age that if they really want to see their mother they'll do so anyway.'

'But they've never said they want to see her.'

'They don't want to hurt you. I know exactly how they feel. When my father left, I desperately wanted to see him, but it upset my mother dreadfully so in the end I saw him very rarely. All too often it's the children who end up as the pawns in the battle between their parents. I dare say you've been worried that if you let them go they may want to stay with their mother?'

He looked surprised then for a moment almost sheepish at her perceptiveness. 'Yes, I suppose I was,' he admitted at last.

'That's always a possibility, I suppose. But they aren't small children, Paul. Very soon they'll be out in the world, living their own lives, anyway. They love you—that's only too obvious—and they always will, but I think their love for you will grow even stronger if you let them go now and allow them to develop a relationship with their mother. It may, of course, be that they're unable to get along with her—that there's too much time and distance between them—in which case they'll hightail it back here to you. But they'll never hold it against you for preventing them from trying.'

He sat in silence for a long while as if reflecting, leaving Catherine to wonder yet again whether or not she had gone too far. After all, here she was, unmarried and childless and offering advice on raising children to an emminent and highly respected consultant surgeon. What right did she have to do so?

She took a deep breath. 'You're probably wondering what I think gives me the right to talk to you in this way...' she began.

'Not at all.' He shook his head.

'After all, I don't have children of my own so it hardly qualifies me...'

'Maybe not. But you were once a child in a similar situation to my children so I guess that alone gives you a right to give your opinion.'

'The situations *are* suprisingly similar,' she agreed. 'Even down to the theatre connections.'

'Tell me about your father,' he said after a moment.

'He was a professional actor. But it was tough, very tough. He did summer seasons and pantomime, but when the work wasn't there the tension between him and my mother was unbearable. He was away a lot as well, which didn't help.'

'How did the marriage end?'

'He worked the summer season in Great Yarmouth and that was where he met Jilly. She was a dancer. He left my mother for Jilly. They married and have a family of their own. I go and see them occasionally.'

'And your mother? Did she ever marry again?'

'No.' Catherine shook her head. 'You see, with her

it was different. She let go of the bitterness but she never stopped loving him. That's more difficult. Then, of course, she died. I still think she died of a broken heart.'

'So you think it's easier, once you've stopped loving someone, to let go of the bitterness than the other way round?' He raised his eyebrows but there was a trace of amusement in his expression.

'Yes,' Catherine replied. 'I would think it must be much harder to let go of the love.'

It had grown quite dark outside the conservatory whilst they had been talking, and a slight breeze had sprung up stirring the white muslin curtains that hung at the French doors.

'I think,' said Paul, rising to his feet and shutting the doors, 'it's time we went inside. I'll make some coffee.'

Together they went into the sitting-room where at his suggestion Catherine sat down in one corner of the sofa. He disappeared into the kitchen only to return a few moments later with a tray bearing a coffee-pot and cups and saucers. He set the tray down on a low table in front of the sofa and Catherine thought he would sit opposite. But instead he moved round the table and sat beside her where he proceeded to pour the coffee into the tiny gold-rimmed cups.

'Tell me,' he said at last as he passed her a cup, 'how would you have felt if your mother had prevented you from taking part in your theatrical productions?'

'I would have been desperately unhappy. You see, because of my father, I believe it was in my blood. At one time I felt I would have liked to pursue it as a career, but because my mother was so against that because she'd witnessed at first hand the anguish that it can bring in terms of disappointment and unemployment, I didn't.'

'Do you regret that now?'

'Sometimes,' she admitted. 'But I love my nursing and I have my amateur productions, although I have to say there was a time that I resented my mother for holding me back, just as I think Abbie might if you prevent her from pursuing her dream.'

'And how would you have felt if your mother had stopped you from seeing your father at all?'

'Devastated,' she replied simply.

There had been a dream-like quality about the entire evening, from Catherine finding herself unexpectedly alone with Paul, to the white wrought-iron table set for two with its snowy cloth and exquisite tableware, to the scent of jasmine and roses and the soft music and to finding herself close beside him on the sofa. She had the feeling that if someone were to pinch her she would wake up and, as on that other occasion when she had dreamt of him, be left with an overwhelming feeling of loss and disappointment.

But this time was real. This was no dream. Paul was beside her, so close that his leg was touching hers, so close that she caught the scent of him—some musky cologne subtly blended with his own male scent which left her almost weak with longing.

When he'd finished his coffee he leaned back and put one arm behind her along the back of the sofa, not touching her but the gesture somehow protective. Deliriously happy, she set her own cup down on the table.

And it was then that he moved his arm until it rested lightly across her shoulders and almost in the same movement brought his other hand round, gently cupping her face, tilting it towards him.

'Catherine…' His breath caught in his throat as the blue eyes gazed into hers. 'I have the feeling that this is madness and that we may well live to regret it…'

'I won't,' she whispered. She allowed her gaze to move from the depth of his eyes where she felt in danger of drowning to the beautifully chiselled outline of his mouth.

Gently, very gently, with a sense of wonder in his eyes, he traced her features with his fingers. And then slowly he drew closer until at last his lips touched hers.

The kiss was as gentle as the touch of a butterfly's wing, a simple touching of skin. But then, as his arms went around her, her lips parted beneath his and desire flared inside her.

CHAPTER ELEVEN

PAUL'S kiss grew more demanding and as passion finally took over, with a little sigh of utter pleasure Catherine gave herself up to the thrill of the moment. No one had quite kissed her like this before—not Greg, and certainly not any of the other boyfriends she had known. But, then, Paul Grantham couldn't really be classed as a boyfriend. Paul Grantham was in a league of his own.

There was no telling where it would have ended if Paul hadn't at last reluctantly drawn away from her. 'We should go,' he murmured.

'Oh…' Her disappointment must have been only too apparent.

'Theo and Abbie will be back. I'll take you home.'

She stared at him for a moment. There was no one at her cottage. No one there to interrupt them. 'Yes,' she said. 'All right.'

While she straightened the sofa cushions he carried the tray back to the kitchen. Within minutes they were in his car, heading for Langbury.

In the darkness she gazed at his profile. Was this really happening? Was this what she wanted? Deep in her heart she knew it was. She loved this man, would probably have done anything for him at that precise moment.

Be careful, her friend Lizzie had warned. Don't get hurt. But that had been before. Before he'd shown interest in her. Before he'd been kind to her. Before he'd

held her in his arms. Before he'd kissed her. Everything
had changed now. He had wanted her as much as she
had wanted him. She had known that in that all too
brief moment of passion. And here they were now, hur-
tling through the night in his car to her home.

He drew up outside the darkened cottage but didn't
switch off the engine. She had been about to climb out
of the car but she paused and threw him a puzzled
glance.

'You'll come in…?' she asked.

She sensed rather than heard his sigh.
'Catherine…I'm not sure that I should.'

'Why not?'

'There are many reasons.' He spread his hands over
the steering-wheel. 'I would like to, believe me, but…'

'And I would like you to,' she said. Half turning in
her seat, she reached out her hand and gently with her
fingertips touched the corner of his mouth.

He switched off the engine and unclipped his seat
belt. A shiver of anticipation touched Catherine's spine
and she opened the car door and stepped out onto the
road. Seconds later he was following her up the path
to her front door.

Teazer didn't get much of a welcome that night and,
after rubbing himself fruitlessly around Catherine's
legs, he took himself off with his tail in the air into a
dark corner of the garden where the rustlings obviously
offered more in the way of enjoyment than his mistress
was prepared to give.

They got no further than the hallway, where, after
closing the front door behind them, Paul with a groan
drew her roughly into his arms. With a sigh of contentment Catherine wound her arms around his neck

and opened her lips beneath his, her gestures both welcoming and submissive.

Desire, which had hovered beneath the surface all evening, flared again and began its deadly throbbing somewhere deep inside, and as her body strained then melted into his she was left in no doubt as to the state of his own arousal.

Once again it was he who drew back. 'Catherine...' His voice was husky. 'I'm really not sure I should be here with you like this...'

'Why not?' She made no attempt to disentangle her arms from around his neck. 'Neither of us is married...'

'No,' he agreed.

'I know you are in effect my boss—does that bother you?'

'A bit,' he admitted. 'I don't want to be accused of taking advantage of a situation...'

'I would never do that.'

'I'm a fair bit older than you, Catherine...'

'Are you? I hadn't noticed. Besides, what's age? It just means you have more experience, that's all—and that's not something I shall be complaining about.' She smiled in the darkness, and leaning against him, lifted her head and pressed her lips against his.

Helplessly he enfolded her in his arms again and this time there was no restraint. Neither was there any protest when she took his hand and led him up the twisting staircase to her bedroom.

But if it had been her taking the initiative until that moment, after that it all changed and it was he who took command. Kiss followed kiss and passion steadily mounted as Paul found the buttons on the saffron dress and one by one unfastened them, slipping the soft fabric from her shoulders and letting it slide to the floor.

The wispy scraps of lace that were her bra and panties soon followed, and within seconds his own clothes had joined the pool of clothing and they stood naked together before the window which overlooked the moon-lit garden of herbs.

'You are beautiful,' he said simply. 'Quite, quite beautiful.' Gently he ran his hands down the smooth skin of her arms. 'Come,' he added, taking her hand and drawing her towards the bed, 'let me love you.'

Heady with longing and breathless with anticipation, she lay beside him and willingly gave herself up to his love-making.

And it was everything she had imagined it would be. Better even than the dream she'd had when he'd made such tender love to her because, after all, that had only been a dream and this time it was real. This time she shuddered with delight when he caressed her breasts, teasing her with his tongue, arousing her to heights she'd never known existed even in her wildest imaginings.

His own satisfaction he delayed again and again as expertly and with all his skill he brought her to the very peak of her desire, and when at last he finally succumbed to his own passion, he made sure that they soared together and that his fulfillment was also hers.

She lay in his arms when it was over, satiated with happiness. She knew he would have to go soon, back to his family, but she also knew that, whatever followed, she would never regret what had happened between them because even if it never happened again, she would have that one ecstatic memory to carry in her heart for the rest of her life.

If Catherine had loved Paul before that night, she loved him a hundred times more afterwards, and for her the following two weeks passed in a haze. Every experience seemed heightened in some way, every pleasure more intense. The quality of each day was determined by the length of time spent in his company and whether or not there was an opportunity to spend time alone together.

At first she told no one of their unfolding love, not because she was ashamed of what was happening but rather that she wanted to keep him to herself for a while, as if when the world knew she would be forced to share him with others.

Inevitably, though, as the days passed little incidents were noticed, and it came as no real surprise to Catherine when it was Lizzie who tackled her first. Lizzie, who had been absent for a few days on annual leave. It came towards the end of a busy shift when Paul and Simon had come up to the ward after operating to check on the progress of their patients. They were standing together with the two staff nurses in the nurses' station.

'Increase Mrs Wyndham's pain relief to every four hours,' said Paul briefly, looking up from the notes he was studying. 'And keep an eye on her blood pressure—it dropped substantially post-op. Mrs Reynolds hasn't come round properly yet, but when she does one of you can have the pleasure of telling her that I've cleared her Fallopian tubes successfully and there's no reason now why she shouldn't have that family she wants so much.'

He paused and glanced rapidly back through the folders of notes on the desk. 'Well, I think that's all for the moment.' He looked up and briefly allowed his gaze to meet Catherine's. 'Thank you.' He nodded and a smile tugged at the corners of his mouth.

Just for a moment Catherine wondered if he was thinking of the previous night when she had gone to his home while Abbie and Theo had been out and where, in the cool grass beneath the trees that fringed the paddock, in no uncertain terms Paul had shown her that his feelings for her were every bit as intense as hers for him. Then the moment was over and with that slight, characteristic inclination of his head he moved away from the station, followed by Simon.

'All right,' said Lizzie as the two men moved out of earshot. 'Come on, let's have it. What's going on?'

'What do you mean?' Catherine kept her tone light but couldn't bring herself to look at Lizzie.

'Well, it's pretty obvious, at least from where I'm standing, that something is going on between you and our Mr Grantham.'

When Catherine remained silent Lizzie threw her a swift, curious glance. 'I'm right, aren't I?' she demanded, a note of incredulous triumph in her voice. 'There *is* something going on!'

'I didn't want to say anything just yet,' mumbled Catherine. 'It's very early days.'

'But you *are* seeing him?'

'Yes, yes I am seeing him.'

'Oh, boy.' Lizzie glanced at her watch. 'I want to hear all about this. We've almost finished here. Meet me in the canteen in twenty minutes.'

Catherine wasn't sure she wanted to tell Lizzie all about it. She wasn't sure she wanted to tell anyone about what was happening between herself and Paul—it was too precious for that. But on the other hand, she didn't really want to upset Lizzie, so at the end of the shift she found herself sitting at a window table in the staff canteen, watching Lizzie as she carried a tray with a pot of tea and a couple of chocolate bars from the counter.

'Right, so tell me, how did all this happen? And when?' Lizzie sat down and began to set out the cups.

'I'm not sure really.' Catherine shrugged. 'It just happened.'

'Well the last thing you told me was that you'd been to his house to give his daughter a singing lesson and that he'd invited you to stay for a barbeque.'

'Oh, well, yes, a bit more has happened since then,' admitted Catherine sheepishly.

'I don't know, I take a few days' annual leave and when I return I find all hell has been let loose.' Lizzie laughed. 'Honestly, Catherine, I can't turn my back for five minutes.' Suddenly she grew serious. 'I seem to remember warning you to be careful,' she said as she began to pour the tea.

'Yes,' Catherine agreed. 'You did. And, yes, I have been.'

'I'm sure you have—in a practical sense. After all, one can just imagine the headlines in the *Langbury Hospital News*—STAFF NURSE ADMITS SENIOR CONSULTANT IS FATHER OF HER LOVE-CHILD.'

'Lizzie, please!' Catherine protested.

'But what I'm more concerned with,' Lizzie went on calmly, 'is not so much the physical as the emotional. Where do you stand in that respect?'

Catherine took the cup Lizzie passed to her and stared down at the bubbles that had formed on top of the tea, only too aware as she did so that her friend was watching her, waiting for her answer. 'I'm in love with him,' she admitted at last.

'Oh, Catherine.' Lizzie had obviously been holding her breath for she let it go now in one long sigh.

'I can't help it.' Catherine shook her head. 'That's the way it is.'

'And what about him? Does he feel the same way?'

'I hope he does,' she replied quietly.

'And what about his family—where do they stand in all this?'

'What do you mean?' Catherine frowned.

'Well, let's face it, Catherine, he doesn't exactly come free from baggage, does he?'

'They seem OK.' Catherine shrugged. 'In fact, at one point I got the distinct impression that they were matchmaking—Abbie, at least.'

'And how about the blonde bombshell?' Lizzie raised one eyebrow. 'What's her reaction?'

'I don't know.' Catherine admitted. 'To tell you the truth, I haven't seen her since that night of the barbeque. I heard someone say she's away, visiting someone.'

'So have you found out exactly who she is?'

'Not really. Only that she's a friend of the family and that I think she lives nearby.'

'Hmm.' Thoughtfully Lizzie topped up her cup then stirred the tea. 'I would say she needs to be watched. Have you tackled Mr Grantham about her?'

'No.' Catherine shook her head. She didn't add that she hadn't done so because she'd been afraid what she might hear. She'd already had the strong feeling that Faye Elton was important in Paul's life in some way, and she feared to know just how important.

'So where do you think this relationship is going?' asked Lizzie curiously as she sipped her tea.

'It's much too soon to say,' Catherine protested. 'It's still at the stage where we're just enjoying being in each other's company.'

'Does the age difference bother you?'

'Not at all. Besides, it isn't that big a difference.'

They sat in silence for a few moments then Lizzie spoke again. 'Did you know that Julian Farnbank is getting up a party from here for the first night of *Oliver!*?'

Catherine looked up in surprise. 'No, I didn't—that's nice.'

'How are the rehearsals going?'

'Pretty well—you know, the usual problems as the opening night approaches.'

'I suppose you'll be going with Paul Grantham?'

'Not really. He's coming, certainly—but I'll be backstage, offering moral support.'

'How things have changed since you first came here, Catherine. D'you remember, Paul Grantham was threatening to withdraw his daughter from the show then and now, well, it's almost beyond belief what has happened.'

'I know,' Catherine admitted. 'At times I can hardly believe myself what has happened. I have to pinch myself to prove it isn't all just a dream!'

'Tell me,' mused Lizzie after a while, 'what's been happening with Lauren while I've been away—have she and Simon got it together again?'

'Well, I thought they had.' Catherine frowned, wrinkling her nose. 'But a couple of nights ago I saw Simon with that new ward clerk—you know, the tall, red-haired girl.'

'That's the trouble with Simon,' Lizzie sighed. 'He loves them then leaves them. Good job you got shot of him, Catherine, he'd have done the same to you.'

'I know.' Catherine pulled a face. 'And that's not all either. I heard he's moving on.'

'What do you mean, moving on?' Lizzie looked puzzled. 'He's always moving on.'

'No, I mean leaving Langbury. Apparently, he's taken a post at a hospital in Swindon.'

'You surprise me. I thought all he wanted was to work with the great Paul Grantham. Well, that's another reason why it's for the best you didn't get involved with him.'

'You're right.' Catherine nodded. 'And I dare say Lauren's thinking the same thing.'

The next few evenings, in the build-up to the opening night of *Oliver!*, were taken up with one rehearsal after another, and, apart from briefly at work, Catherine hardly saw Paul at all. On the night before the opening they spoke on the phone.

'Full dress rehearsal tonight, I understand?' he said.

'Yes, Paul, I'm afraid so...' She held her breath. Maybe he would suggest meeting afterwards. They would have to take Abbie home first, of course, but later... Perhaps a quiet drink somewhere, and then...

'Never mind. The big night tomorrow. Abbie is beside herself.'

'You will be there, won't you?'

'Of course.' His reply was instantaneous. 'I know you won't be able to sit with us, but Abbie tells me there will be a celebratory drink afterwards in the theatre bar. I suggested we all go to an hotel or somewhere but she said that wouldn't be the same at all.'

'She's absolutely right.' Catherine chuckled.

'So I guess I'll just have to wait till then before I see you again. You're off duty tomorrow, aren't you?'

'Yes, I'm taking an annual leave day.'

'And I shall be working at home. I have a clinic for my private patients.'

'I'll see you in the theatre, then.'

He laughed. 'A very different sort of theatre.'

They hung up shortly after that, after Paul had said goodnight and told her to take care. As Catherine replaced the receiver she found herself wishing desperately that she was seeing him that night. She wasn't sure she could wait until after the show the following night, but he hadn't suggested anything. She would just have to be patient, but she couldn't help wondering what he was doing that night that could be so important.

And later, after the dress rehearsal, which went like every other dress rehearsal in every other amateur production she had ever taken part in—with Rod Janes only narrowly avoiding a complete nervous breakdown—she was to wonder even more when it was Theo who picked Abbie up from the theatre and not her father.

She saw the boy briefly in the car park before Abbie got into his car.

'Hello, Theo, nice to see you.' She struggled to hide her disappointment, wondering if he would say why his father hadn't come.

'How did it go?' Theo glanced apprehensively at his sister.

'Awful!' Abbie flounced into the car, collapsing on the passenger seat. 'I was absolutely dreadful. The music was screechy, the dancers were out of step and the timing was all wrong in the final scene.'

'In that case, I don't know whether I'll bother coming tomorrow,' said Theo, pulling a face. 'Maybe I'll wait till later in the week.'

'Oh, it'll all be all right on the night.' It was Catherine who answered but with more optimism than she was feeling. 'Just you wait and see.'

'Abbie, please, keep still. I can't put this eye shadow on properly if you keep on jigging about.'

'Sorry, Catherine.' Abbie closed her eyes. 'I'm so nervous. Honestly, I'm beginning to wish I'd never started this.'

'You don't mean that,' said Catherine calmly. 'You'll be just fine when you get out there, and the audience is going to love you.'

It was the following night and the build-up of tension backstage had almost reached crescendo proportions as costumes were put on, make-up was applied and the dreaded but equally longed-for moment of curtain-up approached.

'There are thousands of people out there!' cried one of the dancers as she erupted into the dressing room. 'I've just peeped through the curtains—honestly, it's dead scary!'

'Thousands?' Catherine had moved from Abbie to another girl who was waiting for help with her make-up.

'Well, hundreds,' the dancer admitted. 'But it seemed like thousands and it's still scary.'

'Of course it's scary,' said Catherine. 'It always is. And if you weren't nervous there would be something wrong because you wouldn't be producing sufficient adrenalin to get you through. You have to take a deep breath, go out there and give the audience what they want. But quite apart from that, you have to enjoy it. Because if you aren't enjoying it, it will show and the audience will know. So off you go, all of you. Relax, and enjoy yourselves. Oh, and, of course—break a leg!'

'Where will you be, Catherine?' asked Abbie anxiously.

'I shall be in the wings, watching you,' Catherine replied.

The atmosphere backstage was electric as the auditorium filled up, the orchestra began tuning their instruments and the beginners took their places on stage. Rod Janes, resplendent in silk shirt and bow-tie, finally stopped rushing around and joined Catherine in the wings.

Catherine had peeped through the curtains but had been unable to pick out Paul and Theo in the audience. But they were there, she knew that, and it gave her a warm glow to know that she had been partly responsible for kindling Paul's interest in his daughter's achievements.

The orchestra went into the intro of the show's most popular music, the lights dimmed and the rustlings ceased in the auditorium as the latecomers stumbled to their places and settled down. And at last came the moment they had all been working towards and waiting for as the curtain rose on the Langbury Amateur Dramatic Society's summer production of Lionel Bart's *Oliver!*

'Darling, you were marvellous!'

'Well done!'

'What a show!'

'Who was that girl?'

'The flower-seller…what an incredible voice!'

'We'll be seeing her in the West End before long—you mark my words! Lloyd Webber will be after her.'

'That's you they're talking about!' Catherine hugged Abbie then together, with the buzz of congratulation ringing in their ears, they began fighting their way through the crush in the bar. She saw the group from the hospital—Julian, who waved to them, Lauren, Tiffany and some of the others. Not Lizzie, because she was on duty that night. Neither was there any sign of Simon, or his latest conquest, although it was difficult to be sure exactly who was, or wasn't, there in that throng of people.

There was, however, no doubting the praise for Abbie. She had stolen the show, just as Catherine had predicted she would, and everyone was well aware that night they had seen a star in the making.

'There's Dad!' Abbie forged on through the crowd, and as people moved aside Catherine caught her first glimpse of him.

Tall, proud and achingly handsome in evening dress, he turned from the bar and his eye caught Catherine's. Briefly he had time only to smile before Abbie hurled herself into his arms.

'Darling,' he said above the hubbub, 'you were wonderful. Just wonderful. I'm so proud of you.'

She was aware of Abbie's flushed face, her radiant happiness, of Theo, a broad grin on his handsome features, equally proud of his talented sister, wanting to share her happiness. It was only then that she realised that the pair of them weren't alone. A third figure, tall and aloof, elegant in a simple black dress, her blonde hair caught up in a jewelled clasp, was standing beside them.

Catherine's heart gave a painful thud of recognition as she realised it was Faye Elton.

CHAPTER TWELVE

PAUL bought drinks for Abbie and herself but Catherine was only really aware of the sense of misery that was growing in the pit of her stomach. Faye was back from wherever it was she'd been, but what was she doing here with Paul? Why had he invited her to accompany him? And why was she standing there so coolly confident, with her arm slipped through his in that maddeningly proprietorial way she had and with that barely veiled look of triumph in her green eyes?

Had she only got back that night, or had she returned the previous day and had she been the reason that Paul had made no attempt to see her, Catherine, the night before? Had they been together then as they were now?

As the questions began to churn in her brain she felt the misery rise from her stomach like bile and threaten to overwhelm her. Blindly she turned and set her glass down on the bar and then, only vaguely aware of an anxious glance from Theo, she groped her way to the ladies.

Inside the cubicle she thankfully pressed her forehead against the cold tiles and desperately attempted to regain control. This was Abbie's night and she mustn't do anything to mar that in any way.

With that thought uppermost in her mind Catherine braced herself and finally stepped from the cubicle, only to find that Faye had come into the ladies and was repairing her already flawless make-up.

Her eyes met Catherine's in the mirror above the line

of wash-basins. 'Theo was concerned about you so I said I'd come and check.'

Catherine gritted her teeth, noticing how she'd said Theo had been concerned and not Paul. 'I'm fine, thank you,' she replied tersely.

'It was probably the heat. These places are all the same—this country can't seem to get its act together over air-conditioning. Not like Spain—the villa's deliciously cool.'

'Is that where you've been?' The question was out before she could help herself.

'My sister needed to convalesce after an operation.' She shrugged. 'It was the obvious choice. It was only pressure of work that prevented Paul from coming with us. Still, never mind, he's already said he'll be able to get away a little later in the year. By that time my sister won't need looking after.'

Her meaning—that she and Paul would be alone at his villa—was only too clear, and as she applied fresh lipstick and pressed her lips together, Catherine swallowed and looked away, her misery refuelled.

There was no telling what would have happened next—whether Catherine would have accompanied Faye back to join the others, whether she would have been invited back to the house to continue celebrating or, if she had, whether she would even have accepted—because at that moment there came a sound from behind the closed door of the end cubicle.

'What was that?' Faye turned, her lipstick poised in her hand. 'It sounded like someone groaning.'

'I don't know.' Catherine frowned. Quickly she made her way to the cubicle and tapped on the door. 'Hello?' she called. 'Are you all right?' A moment of silence was followed by another groan. 'Can you un-bolt the door?' Catherine added urgently.

There came a scrabbling sound then the drawing of the bolt, followed by a dull thud. Catherine began pushing the door but couldn't open it fully because whoever was behind it was by this time slumped on the floor. She did, however, manage to get her head around the door. With a sense of shock she realised that the young woman on the floor was Lauren Keating.

'Lauren…?' she gasped. 'What is it? Whatever is wrong?'

'I don't…know… Terrible pains…' Lauren was bathed in sweat.

'Where?' Catherine demanded. 'Where are the pains?' By this time she'd managed to ease the door fully open so she could crouch beside Lauren. The girl's skin felt cold and clammy to her touch.

'Stomach…' Lauren gasped. 'Low down…very low.'

'Is she drunk?' demanded Faye, looking over Catherine's shoulder.

'No, of course she isn't drunk.' Catherine turned impatiently and saw the disdainful look on Faye Elton's features.

'Drugs, then? You do hear about these things in public loos…'

'Faye, will you go and get Paul?'

'Paul? But he can't come in here. This is the Ladies.'

'Just do as I say,' snapped Catherine. 'Lauren is ill. Get Paul.'

'Oh, very well.'

She never knew what Faye said to him but within moments Paul was there beside her and somehow, between them, they eased Lauren out of the cubicle.

Even before he had questioned or examined Lauren Paul handed Catherine his mobile phone. 'Get an ambulance, Catherine,' he said. 'I don't like the look of this. Lauren's not one to make an unnecessary fuss.'

He took complete control, calmly and gently talking to Lauren, covering her with a rug that one of the theatre staff produced, while Catherine sponged the girl's face, sitting beside her, reassuring her and holding her hands when the pain gripped her.

People came and went—the staff from the theatre, a concerned Julian and Tiffany and a frightened Abbie.

'What's the matter with her, Daddy?' she whispered.

'I'm not sure yet,' Paul replied. 'But she's a member of my team and I want to go with her to the hospital. I shall take the car. Ask Theo to phone for a cab to take Faye and yourselves home.'

'Is that really necessary, Paul?' asked Faye, but no one answered her. 'What about you, Catherine?' asked Abbie.

'I shall go with Lauren in the ambulance,' Catherine replied.

The paramedics arrived and seemed surprised to find that not only was there a senior consultant surgeon on the scene but that the patient was a member of his staff, and the young woman who was to accompany her to hospital was also a registered general nurse.

'Doesn't look as if we're needed here, Neil,' the driver said to his paramedic as they carried Lauren out of the theatre to the waiting ambulance.

Catherine's first concern was for Lauren, but underlying her anxiety was that gnawing sense of misery that wasn't just going to go away without being dealt with. But she knew it would have to wait, have to be put on one side while this very real drama was being played out.

In the ambulance, while Paul followed behind in his Jaguar, Lauren clung to Catherine's hand as wave after wave of pain assailed her.

'We'll soon be there, Lauren,' she murmured reassuringly. 'You're going to be just fine.'

'I don't…feel fine…' Lauren gasped. 'The…pain… is…is terrible.'

On arrival at the hospital, on Paul's instructions, Lauren was taken straight to the gynae ward where she was admitted by an astonished Lizzie who was on night duty.

After Paul had carried out a full examination he asked that Lauren be prepared for emergency surgery and given a pre-med.

'Luckily she didn't have any tea,' said Lizzie as two of the on-duty staff carried out the necessary preparations and blood samples were taken from Lauren for cross-matching. 'It seems she's been feeling off colour for most of the day. Her pulse is high and her blood pressure has dropped.' She glanced at Catherine. 'You know Mr Grantham suspects an ectopic pregnancy?'

Catherine nodded. 'I must confess I'd thought the same. But you can never be sure, of course. It could be appendicitis or even an ovarian cyst.'

'Do you think Lauren knows?'

'Well, she knows the chances, the same as we do…but…' Catherine shrugged.

'Will you stay?' Lizzie asked.

'Yes, I will. I promised Lauren I would, at least until she comes round. I'll go in and sit with her—if that's all right with you, Staff Nurse Rowe?' She managed a faint smile.

'Be my guest,' said Lizzie. 'We've been rushed off our feet tonight.'

Catherine slipped into the curtained cubicle where a single dim light was burning over the bed. Lauren, dressed in a white theatre gown and devoid of jewellery and make-up, was resting quietly, her pain under control with the analgesics she'd been given. An intravenous infusion had been set up and a NIL BY MOUTH sign pinned to the bed rail above a second notice that stated that Mr Grantham was her consultant.

'I never thought it would be me lying in one of these beds, waiting to go to Theatre.' Lauren's gaze met Catherine's and she managed a wan smile.

'Just goes to show we staff are as vulnerable as the next person.' Catherine sat down beside the bed. 'Lauren, is there anyone you'd like me to phone for you?'

'Lizzie phoned my mum—she's on her way,' Lauren replied. She was silent for a while, staring at the ceiling, and Catherine noticed a tear trickle down the side of her face and disappear into her hair. Wordlessly she handed her a tissue from the box on top of the locker.

'You know what this is, don't you?' Lauren said at last.

'Not really. There are a number of things it could be…'

'No.' Lauren shook her head. 'I've missed a period and Mr Grantham says he's pretty certain it's an ectopic.'

'I'm sorry, Lauren.' Catherine took hold of the girl's hand and squeezed it. 'I really am.'

'It was his, Simon's…' she said at last.

'You don't have to tell me this, you know…'

'No, it's OK. I want to.' She wiped her eyes again. 'It was that night...'

'What night?' Catherine frowned.

'The night he went out with you.'

'With me?' For one moment Catherine was startled.

'Yes.' Lauren gulped. 'You and he had had a meal together in the Cat and Fiddle, then...then...you went home. I arrived just as you were leaving and Simon offered to buy me a drink. He seemed in rather a strange mood...not angry exactly, but not particularly happy either. We sat and talked for a time then he offered to drive me home. I agreed...and when we got there, he came in—we had been out together before, you know—and, well, it was like old times and...one thing led to another... You can guess the rest.'

'Oh, Lauren...'

'I thought everything was going to be all right after that, I really did, especially after you told me that you and he weren't an item.'

Catherine remained silent as she remembered how Simon had persisted in his pursuit of her even after that night.

'Then the next thing I knew he was seeing that new ward clerk. Honestly, Catherine, I've been such a fool. But I loved him, you see, and after that night I thought...I really thought...' The tears flowed down her face.

'Lauren, please. Try not to upset yourself.' Catherine paused. 'Do you...do you want to see him? Simon, I mean? I could phone him at his digs.'

'No.' Her reply, in spite of her distress, was emphatic. 'I don't want him to know about this. Ever. He used me, Catherine, that's all it was. I should have had more sense. But this will be over after tonight and he's leaving Langbury very soon anyway.'

'I know…but I don't see why he should get away with it—'

'No, Catherine.' Lauren's eyelids began to close as wearily she gave in to the effects of the pre-med.

'All right.' Catherine nodded and squeezed the girl's hand again. 'If that's the way you want it.'

It was very late when Catherine finally left the hospital. She'd stayed until Lauren was safely through the operation, albeit after losing the embryo and one Fallopian tube, and until her mother had arrived to take over at the girl's bedside.

She called a cab while Paul was still talking to Lauren's mother and was on her way home before he'd had the chance even to change out of his theatre greens. In spite of the heaviness of her heart, that was the way she wanted it. If she'd waited, there was no doubt he would have offered to run her home, but then what? A polite goodnight outside her cottage?

Leaning her head back, she closed her eyes.

Her brain was in turmoil and she hardly knew where to start to untangle her thoughts. Maybe tonight, with total exhaustion threatening, she shouldn't even try. Maybe it would be far simpler to just drift away into blessed oblivion.

'Bad news, love?'

Catherine opened her eyes and saw that the cab driver was watching her in his mirror. 'I'm sorry?' she asked.

'I was just wondering if you'd had bad news. Usually when I get a call to the hospital at this time of night it's one of two things—a death or a birth. I figured it probably wasn't a birth...'

'Er, no.' She hesitated. 'It was a friend...she had to have an emergency operation.'

'Is she OK?' He sounded genuinely concerned.

'Oh, yes.' Catherine nodded wearily. 'She'll be fine now.'

'My brother had to have an emergency operation once—on his heart. He's OK now. Marvellous what they can do these days, isn't it?'

Catherine agreed that, yes, it was. Maybe, she thought, that was what she needed. Emergency surgery to her heart.

Her cottage was in darkness when she arrived but after she'd paid the driver who obligingly waited until she'd unlocked her front door and switched on a light—'Can't be too careful these days, love'—her phone started to ring. Closing the front door behind her, she picked up the receiver.

'Catherine.'

'Paul.'

'How did you get home?'

'I called a cab.'

'What in the world did you do that for? I would have taken you home.'

'It was very late and you must be tired,' she heard herself say not wanting to give him the real reason—that she couldn't have borne it.

'Even so. There was no need.'

'Is Lauren all right?'

'Yes. At least physically. I'm not sure about emotionally.'

'I know. She told me.' She took a deep breath. 'Paul, I'm very tired.'

'Yes, of course. Will I see you tomorrow?'

'I don't think so, Paul.'

'But it's Sunday. I was hoping you would come over for lunch then perhaps—'

'No, Paul. I don't think that would be a good idea in the circumstances.' Quietly she replaced the receiver then lifted it again and set it on the table so that the phone was off the hook.

If Lauren had considered herself to have been a fool, then she, Catherine, had surely been doubly so. With a heart that was close to breaking she stared around her tiny cottage at her simple furniture, her precious bits and pieces. How could she have ever thought, even for a moment, that she could fit into Paul's life?

They were worlds apart.

He had even voiced his fears—tried to warn her that it wouldn't work. But she had been blinded by love, telling him that the age difference didn't matter, that none of the differences mattered. And perhaps, to a certain extent, that was still true. Even the fact that he'd been married and had a family of his own could surely have been overcome, but the one thing she had under-estimated had been the importance of Faye Elton in his life.

She had hoped, in her naïvety, her innocence, that any previous or existing relationship he might have had would have ceased once they had slept together. Like Lauren, she had hoped that would solve everything. What a fool she'd been.

With tears in her eyes she stood up and walked into the kitchen. Teazer was curled up in the rocking chair, fast asleep. He opened one eye, looked at her, then yawned, stood up, turned round a couple of times and settled down again with his back to her. Even he didn't want to know.

She'd told herself that if she slept with Paul she would never regret it, that even if nothing else happened she would be able to live on the memory of that one time. What she hadn't bargained for was that she would end up loving him even more.

She'd even thought that Faye Elton had disappeared off the scene, that in some way she'd ceased to be important to Paul. The truth was very different for not only had Faye simply been away with her sister, they had been at Paul's villa in Spain, somewhere Faye was obviously very much at home, somewhere she had, no doubt, been many times before, somewhere she would go many times again.

With a final glance at Teazer's uncompromising back, and choking back her tears, Catherine switched off the kitchen light and made her way up the stairs to bed.

Something had woken her. She turned over and lay on her back, listening. Sunlight was streaming into the bedroom and through the gap in the curtains she could see a patch of blue sky. It looked as if it was going to be a beautiful day.

Then memory flooded back and she groaned.

Downstairs, Teazer was miowing loudly but she didn't think it was that which had woken her. She sat up and stretched, then her doorbell sounded and she knew that had been the sound which had penetrated her sleep.

With a muttered exclamation she swung her legs to the floor and grabbed her towelling robe. It must be the postman. She was halfway down the stairs, had

seen Teazer prowling about in the hall and the dark
outline of a figure through the stained-glass panel on
her front door, before she remembered it was Sunday.
Most other things happened on Sundays nowadays but
there was still no postal service as far as she knew.

She unlocked the door and tugged it open, half expecting to see one of her neighbours on the step. So
the shock was even greater than it might have been to
see Paul standing there, leaning against the doorframe,
a supermarket carrier bag in one hand. He looked cool
and handsome in cream chinos and an open-necked
shirt. She stared at him in horrified amazement.

CHAPTER THIRTEEN

'Hi,' PAUL said. 'Did I wake you?'

It was obvious that this must have been the case, and Catherine was suddenly only too aware of how she must look with her hair all over the place, her face heavy with sleep and wearing her oldest bathrobe.

'I've brought breakfast,' he said when, still speechless, she continued to stare at him. 'I think, however, it might be a bit difficult to eat it out here on the step.'

Wordlessly she stood aside and let him in, closing the door behind him, hoping in that instant that the old couple opposite hadn't seen him arrive. With a little shudder she followed him into the kitchen.

He'd set the bag on the table and was unpacking its contents—croissants, a French stick, a jar of preserves, peaches and fresh orange juice. Teazer was rubbing himself hopefully around Paul's legs.

'I thought we'd go Continental,' he said with a smile. 'Shall I put some coffee on?'

The mention of the Continent reminded Catherine of Spain and seemed to galvanise her out of her stupor. 'The coffee-beans are in that jar.' She pointed to a shelf. 'And the percolator is over there. Just give me ten minutes to shower and dress.' She fled, out of the kitchen and up the stairs, Teazer at her heels, leaving Paul to make the coffee and warm the croissants.

Her mind was racing while she showered and washed her hair. What was he doing here at this ungodly hour on a Sunday? Why had he come? Surely he must have been relieved that she'd apparently got the message where he and Faye were concerned. Wasn't he glad to have been let off the hook? Weren't all men pleased when they were excused from painful confrontation?

Quickly she towel-dried the excess water from her hair then combed it back behind her ears. She was thankful that the summer sun had tanned her face, in spite of the smattering of freckles across her nose, because there was no time to apply any make-up. Finally she pulled on a pair of shorts and a sleeveless pink top then, with her heart thumping, she took a deep breath and made her way downstairs.

He had set the table and a delicious smell of coffee and freshly warmed croissants drifted through the cottage. He'd opened the back door and was sitting on a wooden garden chair in the sunshine, surrounded by the terracotta flowerpots she'd planted with geraniums and trailing lobelia.

He glanced over his shoulder as she approached. 'I was just admiring your garden,' he said, 'but now that you're here, I'll pour the coffee.'

It was all so matter-of-fact and he was so casual that an onlooker who didn't know could be forgiven for thinking that they did this every Sunday morning.

But Catherine wasn't an onlooker. She knew better. She waited until they were seated at the table, until he'd poured the orange juice and the coffee and was spreading his croissant with the rich cherry preserve.

'Why have you come, Paul?' she said at last.

'I decided after last night we needed to talk,' he replied calmly.

She shrugged. 'I can't see that there's anything to say.'

'I disagree. I would say there's everything to say. To be honest, I can't understand what's changed in so short a space of time. A couple of days ago everything between us was wonderful, or at least I thought it was…'

'So did I,' Catherine replied tersely.

'So what happened?'

She stared at him. Did he really not know? Could he really be so insensitive? 'Faye Elton happened,' she retorted.

'Faye Elton?' He frowned. 'I don't understand. What's she got to do with it?'

'Well, for a start, she came back from holiday.'

'Yes.' He nodded. 'So what?'

Catherine took a deep breath. 'Can we stop playing games, Paul?' she said.

'I wasn't aware that we were.'

Trying to ignore the puzzled expression in his eyes, she carried on. 'Faye spoke to me at the theatre. She left me in no doubt about her relationship with you.'

'Her relationship with me…?' He stared at her, the blue eyes widening in astonishment.

'She made it plain that she'd been staying in your villa in Spain, that she'd been there many times before and that she intended—'

'She said that?' Swiftly he interrupted, cutting her short, taking her by surprise.

'Well, yes…'

'Catherine, Faye Elton has certainly been to Spain— with her sister I believe—but they weren't staying at my villa.'

'Weren't they?' Catherine frowned, momentarily thrown.

'No, as far as I know, they were staying with friends

in their villa which is about twenty kilometres away from mine.'

'Oh.' For a moment Catherine was lost for words.

'And as for her saying she'd visited my villa in the past, well, that's true, but it was only once for drinks, and that was when the friends she was staying with came to visit neighbours of mine and I invited them over. It was how I met Faye. In conversation it transpired that we both came from the same part of the country. She actually lives in Woodstock. I told her I was looking for a temporary secretary to help me with my private patients because my regular secretary, Mo, has been on long-term sick leave and she agreed to step in and fill the breach.'

'Oh,' said Catherine again. 'I thought…I thought… Oh, I don't know quite what I thought…' She trailed off, uncertain how to continue.

'You thought she and I were an item, didn't you?' said Paul quietly at last.

'Well…'

'Go on, you can say.'

'Well, yes, I did,' she admitted. 'It did rather look that way, Paul. She was there…at the house, and she seemed so…so…'

'At home?' He raised one eyebrow.

'Well, yes. But then she disappeared, and you and I…happened…but then suddenly she was back and she was there beside you at the theatre last night, and I realised she'd actually been home the night before…when I hadn't seen you…and then she told me about Spain and, well, there was definitely something in her manner that was warning me off.'

'And you thought what had happened between you and I had been just because she was away?'

Catherine allowed her gaze to meet his. 'I didn't know quite what else to think, Paul,' she replied quietly.

He inhaled deeply. 'The only reason she was with us at the theatre was because she came to the house on her return from Spain and Abbie asked her if she intended coming to the show. Faye said she feared she might have left it too late to get a ticket then Abbie told her about the spare ticket I had bought.'

'Spare ticket?' Catherine frowned.

He nodded. 'Even though you'd said you would be busy backstage I lived in hopes that you would be able to join Theo and me so that we could all watch Abbie together.'

For a moment Catherine couldn't speak because a lump had suddenly risen in her throat.

'Mind you,' said Paul with a sudden chuckle, 'Abbie wasn't very popular with Theo for that.'

'Oh?' said Catherine faintly, finding her voice from somewhere.

'Theo can't stand Faye—he calls her the Preying Mantis.' Paul chuckled again then, in silence, finished his croissant before picking up the coffee-pot and topping up her cup. 'Faye means nothing to me, Catherine. She wanted there to have been something and I believed I'd made it plain to her that there never would be. Maybe I hadn't made it plain enough but I'll make sure she knows the score now. While we're on the subject,' he went on after a moment, 'you need have no fears about the night before last either. I was otherwise engaged, but it had nothing to do with Faye, I can assure you.'

'Paul…' Suddenly she felt horribly embarrassed. How could she have dared to question his motives or what he did in his private life? 'You don't have to tell me…' she managed to continue at last.

'It's OK.' He shrugged, apparently casually, but she had the impression that somehow he was as keyed up as she was. 'I want you to know. For a good part of the evening I was talking to my ex-wife.'

She stared at him in astonishment, hardly able to believe what she was hearing.

'We talked at great length,' he went on, 'and the outcome was that when she comes to England in a couple of weeks' time to visit her mother Theo and Abbie are going to see her.'

'Oh, Paul…'

'And if all goes well during that meeting,' he went on, 'they are going to the States next month for a visit.'

'Paul, that's marvellous.' She set her cup down and stared at him across the table. 'But what made you change your mind?'

'You did,' he replied simply.

'I did?' her eyes widened. 'But I didn't do anything.'

'Oh, Catherine, you really don't have any idea, do you?' Gently he shook his head and it seemed for a moment as if he had difficulty in continuing. 'You came along and into my life like a breath of fresh air,' he went on at last. 'You made me take a long, cool look at myself. And you know something? I didn't like what I saw.'

'No?' she whispered.

He shook his head. 'I'd become a rigid and bitter man who was becoming thoroughly set in his ways, and my bitterness was rubbing off on the children and having a terrible influence on them. When my wife left me I couldn't see beyond the fact that she'd preferred another man to me. I couldn't see that I might have been partly to blame for working every hour that God gave, never spending any time with her or the children and taking no interest in anything she did.'

'Yours must have been a terribly demanding career,' said Catherine slowly.

'It was,' he agreed. 'But that was no excuse. I also had a wife and children with needs of their own. I should have seen the warning signs, but I didn't. After she'd gone I believed she'd forfeited any rights to see the children. It was you who persuaded me otherwise. Abbie was on the brink of rebellion because of my completely unfounded prejudice of the theatre. I'd considered the theatre to have been responsible for the break-up of my marriage and I was refusing to acknowledge Abbie's talent, while Theo was well on the road to anarchy. Probably all they were in need of was a softening of my attitude and some contact with their mother.'

'It may not all be as simple as that,' said Catherine slowly.

'I know that,' he agreed. 'We have a long way to go to put things right, but it'll be a start. And I have to say I can't believe how much better I feel for simply letting go of my anger and resentment. I tell you, Catherine, you came along and turned our lives upside down, and before I knew where I was I was falling headlong in love with you.'

Helplessly she stared at him, hardly able to believe what she was hearing. 'Why didn't you say?' she whispered at last.

'Because I didn't think I stood an earthly chance, that's why, and I wasn't certain I could cope with a mighty dose of rejection.' Paul pulled a face.

'But why should you think you wouldn't stand a chance?' She frowned.

'We are two very different people.'

'I know,' she admitted. '*I* was afraid of that.'

'I thought our worlds would simply collide. There's you, young and lovely with your whole life before you. You will want to marry and have children. And then there's me, at my age with a ready-made family, complete with teenage traumas. Honestly, Catherine, I didn't think you'd look twice at me, especially with competition around like Simon Andrews...'

'Oh, Paul!' With a sound that was a cross between a sigh and a sob she stood up and, rounding the table, flung her arms around him. Teazer, startled out of his wits by the sudden activity, leapt out of the rocking chair where he had been happily washing himself and streaked out into the garden. 'I didn't think you'd want *me*...'

'Why ever would you think that?' In amazement he pulled her onto his lap.

'I didn't think you'd look twice at me,' she protested.

'But why?' he looked puzzled.

'Well, there you were—my boss really, an eminent and highly respected consultant surgeon at the very peak of your career with a lifestyle that's, well, quite frankly out of this world compared to what I'm used to. And then there's me, a lowly little staff nurse. And then there was Faye Elton...'

'I told you—'

'Yes, you did. I know now, but at the time all I saw was a rich, glamorous blonde and I automatically thought that she was the type of woman you were attracted to.'

He chuckled then, lifting his head, he drew her face down until his lips brushed hers. 'So am I in with a chance, then?'

'I don't see why not.' Taking his face between her hands, she allowed his mouth to claim hers.

'Would you want children?' Paul asked.

It was much later and they lay together in Catherine's bed in the glorious aftermath of love-making.

'I'd always thought I would one day…but I dare say Abbie and Theo would keep me fully occupied…'

'I probably wouldn't take too much persuading to start again.'

Raising herself onto one elbow, she looked down at him in delighted amazement. 'Do you really mean that?' she asked.

'Well, you know us gynae men where babies are concerned.' He grinned. 'And, besides, I wouldn't be able to resist the idea of having a baby with you.'

With a little sigh of contentment she snuggled down again beside him then she gave a sudden gurgle of mirth.

'What are you laughing at?'

'I was just imagining telling Sister Marlow about us,' she replied. 'She was quite emphatic that she didn't like affairs or liaisons between members of her team. I can't imagine how she'll take this.'

'You just leave Glenda Marlow to me. Besides, ours won't be an affair—you'll be my wife. It makes all the difference in the world.' Paul paused and looking down at her in sudden alarm, said, 'You *will* marry me, won't you, Catherine?'

'Oh, yes. Of course I will. Didn't you think I

would?' she asked when he gave a sigh that sounded suspiciously like one of relief.

'I wasn't sure. There was me automatically assuming it would be what you'd want. But these days who knows? So many don't seem to want marriage but bring up their children regardless.'

'Well, here's one who does,' she said fiercely. 'Want marriage, I mean.'

'So your feeling about coming back to Langbury was right after all,' he said. 'That person with whom you'd want to spend the rest of your life was right here, waiting for you.'

'Yes,' she agreed. 'Maybe I should learn to trust my intuition more than I do.' She paused. 'Can we go and tell Theo and Abbie?'

Not giving him the chance to answer, she added anxiously, 'How do you think they'll take it?'

'They'll be delighted. Abbie thinks the sun shines out of you anyway, and hadn't you noticed that Theo's practically eating out of your hand? However...' Turning over so that his body half covered her, his skin warm against hers, he said, 'I think that can wait for a while. There are far more urgent matters to attend to.'

'Whatever you say, Mr Grantham.' With a sigh of pleasure Catherine lifted her arms, wound them around his neck and drew him down towards her.

MILLS & BOON®

Makes any time special™

Mills & Boon publish 29 new titles every month. Select from...

Modern Romance™   **Tender Romance**™

Sensual Romance™

Medical Romance™ **Historical Romance**™

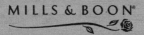

Medical Romance™

ACCIDENTAL RENDEZVOUS *by Caroline Anderson*

Audley Memorial Series

Audley A&E is an emotional place, but Sally is not prepared for the emotions Nick Baker stirs when he comes back into her life. He's been searching for her for seven years, and for all that time Nick's unknowingly been a father...

ADAM'S DAUGHTER *by Jennifer Taylor*

Part 1 of A Cheshire Practice

Nurse Elizabeth Campbell *had* to tell Dr Adam Knight that he was the father of her sister's child. He was furious that no one told him he had a daughter and was determined to be in her life – only that meant he was in Beth's life too. This fuelled their attraction, but were his feelings really for her, or for her sister?

THE DOCTOR'S ENGAGEMENT *by Sarah Morgan*

Holly Foster has been best friends with GP Mark Logan since childhood, so when he asked her to pretend to be his fiancée, how could she refuse? One searing kiss was all it took to make Holly realise that being Mark's fiancée was very different to being his friend!

On sale 7th September 2001

Available at most branches of WH Smith, Tesco, Martins, Borders, Easons, Sainsbury, Woolworth and most good paperback bookshops

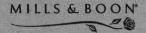

4 Books
and a surprise gift!

We would like to take this opportunity to thank you for reading this Mills & Boon® book by offering you the chance to take FOUR more specially selected titles from the Medical Romance™ series absolutely FREE! We're also making this offer to introduce you to the benefits of the Reader Service™—

- ★ FREE home delivery
- ★ FREE gifts and competitions
- ★ FREE monthly Newsletter
- ★ Books available before they're in the shops
- ★ Exclusive Reader Service discounts

Accepting these FREE books and gift places you under no obligation to buy; you may cancel at any time, even after receiving your free shipment. Simply complete your details below and return the entire page to the address below. *You don't even need a stamp!*

YES! Please send me 4 free Medical Romance books and a surprise gift. I understand that unless you hear from me, I will receive 6 superb new titles every month for just £2.49 each, postage and packing free. I am under no obligation to purchase any books and may cancel my subscription at any time. The free books and gift will be mine to keep in any case.

M1ZEB

Ms/Mrs/Miss/Mr ....Initials..
BLOCK CAPITALS PLEASE

Surname ....

Address ....

....

....Postcode ....

Send this whole page to:
UK: The Reader Service, FREEPOST CN81, Croydon, CR9 3WZ
EIRE: The Reader Service, PO Box 4546, Kilcock, County Kildare (stamp required)